DARE ME

FOR A MILLION DOLLARS

RIVER LAURENT

DARE ME
Published by River Laurent
Copyright © 2017 by River Laurent

ISBN: 978-1-911608-10-3

❀ Created with Vellum

ACKNOWLEDGMENTS

A kiss for…
Leanore Elliott & Brittany Urbaniak

CHAPTER 1

DAKOTA

"What now?" I wail, frustrated beyond belief.

Traffic is crawling at such a snail's pace, I swear, if I get out now and stroll to my interview, I'd probably get there faster. I crane my neck to try and see what the slow down for the last two miles is about.

This whole journey has been a total nightmare. Every single light along City Avenue was red and I kept getting stuck behind buses. It is like there is a Traffic God up there looking down on me and saying, "More stop lights! More taxis. More people who have all the time in the world. More everything. Make Dakota late!"

I glance at myself in the rearview mirror. Damn, my face is already glowing with a thin sheen of sweat. The hour I spent on my hair and makeup, carefully making my hazel eyes pop with pale pink shadow and eyeliner is on the verge of ruin. I tuck a lock of limp strawberry blonde hair behind my ear. Why did I even bother curling it? It looks so pathetic now, like it wants to be all beachy and shiny, but is too lazy to give it much effort. Not that any of this will matter if I don't make it in time for the interview.

I check my car's clock anxiously. Oh God, less than fifteen minutes for my appointment. I have to make it to the studio before somebody decides I'm a no-show.

I close my eyes, take a deep breath, and unclench my hands from the steering whe*el. Calm down, Dakota. You don't want to arrive there a hot mess. Miracles do happen. Everything is going to be fine.* I open my eyes and see that traffic has started moving up ahead, but the slowpoke in front of me is happily chatting away on his cellphone.

I see red. I lower the car window furiously. "What is this? Drive Like a Jerk Day?" I yell at him.

He turns around and gives me a dirty look.

Doesn't matter, I don't back down. "Come on. Move. Please," I yell.

It's not like me to act this way, but this is a life and death situation, and I'm not being dramatic. This interview could change my mother's life. Actually, her very life hinges on the outcome. The traffic speeds up again and I glance at the clock. Less than two minutes left, but I'm almost there. Almost.

"Finally," I breathe out as I show my ID to the guard and turn into the entrance of the parking lot. It's still only ten minutes after nine, so I might be all right. Ten minutes at a high-traffic time has to be acceptable. Right? They have to expect people to be a little late when they're coming in during rush hour.

Seeing a vacant parking space, I immediately put my car into reverse and step on the gas pedal. *Yay, I made it. I'm here.* Quickly, I glance in the rearview mirror. To my relief, my makeup is holding up okay. A quick powder and I should be okay.

Suddenly, something hits my car!

Noooooo....

Two

Dakota

CHAPTER 2

DAKOTA

W here did that shiny silver-blue Cadillac come from? This can't be happening to me.

A tall dark-haired man is out of the Cadillac before I can take another breath. "What the hell is wrong with you?" he shouts, striding around to the front of his car to check out the damage my old Impala has caused to his brand new Caddy. From the stiff angry set of his shoulders, it isn't good news.

I jump out too, ready to knock his head off. Who the hell does this guy think he is? I can do road rage too. I'm not having my head chewed off by any random idiot who can't park. This is not my fault and I'm not going to be bullied into paying for any damages. "What the hell is wrong with me?" I shout hotly. "Maybe if you hadn't come careening in behind me, this wouldn't have happened! That was my parking space."

He straightens and glares at me.

Bad driver but oh wow—drop dead handsome. Yeah, I've locked eyes with the most splendid man I've ever seen in my entire life. And that includes guys inside magazines pages. I stop short and catch my breath. My heart is jumping. Oh God, those eyes. They're the most beautiful shade of glorious azure, like the sky on a clear, autumn day. I can't tear my gaze away from them. I could easily stare into them and forget about my interview, my car, my life. Except those beautiful eyes are filling with irritation.

"What are you talking about? I was halfway into the space when your piece of junk struck me," he says curtly.

What the hell is wrong with me? Why am I drooling like a love-mad teenager over this rude brute? I shake myself free of the spell of his eyes, the chiseled perfection of his features and oh, yeah, the ridiculously fit body under his expensive suit and straighten my spine. This is a battle. "Didn't you see me? There must have been only ten inches between me being all the way into that space when you hit me."

His eyes flash with disbelief. "Ten inches? Are you blind? Look at the position of my car and yours."

Ignoring his scowl, I lift my chin and walk around to the back of my car to inspect the damage for myself. When I do, I let out a laugh of sheer relief.

"You think this is funny?" he asks, following behind me.

I look up.

His face is turning dark with anger.

"No, no, not funny at all." I struggle to keep myself under control. "I'm just relieved."

"Relieved?" he bellows.

Gee. I'm batting a thousand with this guy. "I'm sorry, but it doesn't look like a lot of damage. Does it? I only see two scratches and a slight dent. Your headlight isn't even broken."

Those beautiful eyes narrow into slits. "Listen. Just because you drive a battered old piece of shit and think it's real funny that you knocked some rust off it—"

"Excuse me?" Hot or not, nobody talks to me that way.

"—doesn't mean I should dismiss the damage to my car," he continues like I never spoke at all.

I'm not taking crap from some asswipe on the road. "Oh, stop being such a drama queen. This is hardly damage. I've seen worse done to a car with an out-of-control shopping cart. Consider yourself lucky you got off this easy and maybe, think it through the next time you decide to steal another driver's parking space."

"I didn't steal your space. You tried to steal mine," he growls.

"Really? What's your definition of stealing, then? Because I was nearly parked when you hit me, jackass."

"Oh, very classy."

God, why couldn't he be some ugly smooch, so I can really get mad? "Just because you drive a fancy car doesn't mean you own the world."

"I'm surprised they even allow that piece of junk you're driving, on the road," he says straightening the collar of his snowy white shirt.

"I can't believe you said that," I gasp. What a rude asshole.

"I've said worse," he says dryly.

"We can't all drive around in a Cadillac," I fire back, hands on my hips. It's not easy to get me worked up, but once I am? Forget about it. My Philly comes out, as Mom likes to tease. "Maybe if you'd get your nose out of the air, you'd be a much better driver." I turn around to take a look at my car since I was too busy getting yelled at to examine my own damage. My tail light is busted. Terrific.

He snorts behind me. "How can you tell what damage happened today and what was already wrong with it?"

This guy is unbelievable. I whirl around. "You have to be the biggest douche I've ever met," I snarl, totally losing control of myself. Maybe because I'm already having a crappy day or maybe because he's right. I know my car is a piece of junk. Every time it starts, I consider myself lucky. And worse still, knowing he's way out of my league. He would never give a poor girl like me a second look. People like him think they're above everything and everybody.

"I don't have time for this. It's obvious you won't be able to afford to pay for the damages to my car, so we'll just agree to repair our own cars."

"Don't do me any favors," I say proudly. "I'll take some photographs and let the insurance company decide whose fault it is."

"Oh, for fuck's sake," he mutters, but he takes his mobile phone out of his jacket and quickly takes some shots.

I run around to the driver's seat and do the same.

"Are you finished?" he asks.

"Yes," I say snapping the last photo from an angle that clearly shows that my car is more in the space than his.

"All right. Let's get it over with. Show me your license and I'll show you mine"

"Show me yours first?" I say not liking his tone as I try to ignore his incredibly blue eyes.

"Wow, what a bimbo," he says reaching into the back pocket of his expensive Italian slacks.

"What did you just call me?" I ask, getting a whole lot madder.

"Here's my license," he says ignoring my question.

I snatch it from his fingers and glance down at it. "Oh, it says Trent. I expected it to say Rich Jerk," I note as I glance up smiling sweetly.

I expect him to say something about my license not having Bimbo on it, but he doesn't.

"Here, Dakota," he says dismissively as he hands my license back.

"You're not going to write down my information?" I ask.

"I've already memorized it, but I'm sure you'll need a pen and paper." He pulls a Montblanc pen from his shirt pocket and holds it out for me.

I want to slap the expensive pen out of his hand and go get my Bic pen out of the glove compartment, but I don't. Hell, between lusting after him and establishing that it was his fault… I'd forgotten about my appointment.

"Would you please hurry? I'm late!" he says as I scribble his name and license number on the scrap of paper I found in my pocket.

"Yes, can't let you be late, can we?" I mock, as I hand back his license, and whirl around to leave. I take two steps.

"My pen, please."

Shit. I am such a fool. My whole body goes up in flames of embarrassment. I plaster a fixed smile on my face and turn back. "Oh, yes. Heaven forbid. I'm sure it cost more than I make in a month!"

He takes a sharp breath, like he's ready to let loose with something really good—or, rather bad, but his eyes widen as he remembers something. "Shit. I was already running late and you've just made things worse."

I check my phone. It's now nine-twenty.

He gives me a dark look. "If I lose this opportunity because of you…"

My hands ball into fists. "Me? You lose it because of me?" I splutter. "This is all your fault."

"Why do bimbos always look so damn hot when they're annoyed?"

My eyes widen with shock. Is he flirting with me? I suddenly don't know if I should be ecstatic, he called me damn hot or angry because he called me a bimbo again. I hold up my hand with my middle finger extended.

Trent laughs and shakes his head. "Have a nice day too, Dakota," he says. He locks his car and starts walking away.

I watch him slack-jawed. He's just going to leave his car halfway in MY parking space.

Oh, if he is not the most arrogant, self-satisfied, selfish, uncivilized jerk I have ever met in my life. But I can't stand here cursing him. I'm already twenty-two minutes late for my appointment. I rush back to my Impala. I pull out and look for another parking space. Luckily, only a few yards away, a woman comes out of her space and I quickly dart in. I lock my car and race to the building.

CHAPTER 3

TRENT

Oh! Fuck! Not her again. No way.

"Hold the elevator," she yells as she comes running towards me.

I don't do any such thing. She's already made me late enough. Let her wait for the next one. I'm in a rush, besides I don't want to be trapped in a confined space with this woman. This loud-mouthed, pushy, terrible driver from hell. She slammed into me and had the nerve to tell me it was my damn fault.

I lean back against the wall of the elevator and watch her through half-closed lids. She is incredibly delicious, though. Curves for days. Ahhhh...and all of them bouncing for all their worth.

When she realizes I'm not going to hold the door for her, her expression changes to one of fury. I've never met a girl who looks so hot when she's mad. If we'd met in different circumstances. Maybe if she was gagged or something, I'd love to show her what ten inches really looks like. My fantasy is interrupted when she suddenly throws her purse towards me. The damn thing flies through the open doors and lands next to my feet.

I have no choice.

I kick it out of the elevator.

First her jaw drops, then she starts shouting abuse at me. She really is a very, very sexy spitfire. Instead of giving up like any other normal woman would. She starts running like her life depends on it.

I realize with a sinking heart that she's gonna make it and I'll have to fucking share the elevator with her. I hit the button to close the doors again and to my relief, the doors start to close.

I smile at her.

She responds with another unladylike string of curses.

She's getting close, but I'm not too worried. There are only three inches left before the door completely closes on her. But just as the doors are about to meet, her fingers slide in and slam on the edge of one door.

Oh, for God's sake. Can't I catch a break today? The doors swish open. I can't believe my luck. Like I needed something else to go wrong this morning. It's like watching a horror movie.

She picks up her purse from where I kicked it to and walks in, giving me a murderous glance. Her face is red and her eyes are glittering.

God, she's fucking gorgeous.

"Are you always such a jerk?" she fumes as she moves towards the button panel. Resentment radiates from her in waves.

Like she has any right to be resentful after what she did to my car. "You could always have waited for the next elevator."

"I'm late for an appointment," she informs huffily.

"Thanks to your dramatics. I'll be late for mine too," I say coldly.

She goes to hit her floor number but seeing that it's already lit up, stands stiffly as far away from me as possible. The doors close and we're the only two people in the shiny elevator.

I refuse to look at her. If I do, I might start another fight and I should be focused on how I'm going to score a spot on the show, not whether I should strangle her or kiss that bratty mouth.

I adjust the sleeves of my shirt, making sure they're lined up with the jacket sleeves. Then I brush invisible lint off my chest. Fidgeting. It's what I do when I'm in an uncomfortable situation. I hear a snicker from beside me and refuse to give in, but my eyes slide over.

Nice dress. It shows off her hourglass shape. Her breasts are still heaving. They would look great on top of me.

She catches me looking and I look away. What the fuck is wrong with me?

"Anything I can do for you?" she murmurs sarcastically.

I glance at the twin spots of high color on her cheeks. I don't fancy a slap, so… "No, not a thing," I answer coolly.

"Good, because that's what you'll get."

After that, we ride up to the fifth floor in total silence. When the doors open, I can't get the hell off the elevator fast enough.

There must be at least two hundred people milling about in the hall, waiting their turn in front of the studio audience. The two most important questions they need to answer are…

Do I look good on-camera?

Am I willing to do just about anything for that prize?

I can answer one of those two questions easily. Yes, I look damn good on or off-camera. And yes, I would do just about anything for the money this game show is offering. It's my last chance.

"You here for the audition interview?" A harried looking production assistant approaches me moments after I step into the hallway.

"Yup."

"Right. Get to the back of the line. At the end of the hall," he says rudely, and points.

I look down that hall. That long, long hall. His shitty attitude makes me want to punch him one, but I pull together what's left of my dignity and go to the end. I'm not going to fall at the first hurdle. I need the prize money.

Talk about a sea of humanity. The money has attracted a wide range of people. Most of them have dressed to be remembered. There are costumes, club clothes, even a few people clad all in leather. I bet the girl in a chicken costume

14

is willing to do just about anything for money. I wonder if a suit was the right way to go. Who will remember a suit?

The road hazard is already waiting at the end of the line. She rolls her eyes so hard when she sees me she could do permanent damage. "Oh," she coos sweetly. "You must be in the wrong place. This is the line for the *common* people."

"Cranky little thing, aren't you?" I retort coldly, as I take my place behind her.

She ignores my comment and turns her head to look at me. "I thought you would be here for some big-shot meeting instead of auditioning for a reality game show."

"What a surprise...you were wrong about something."

"Yes, I was, but I have you pegged now." She's all happy now, she made it on time for her appointment, and she is now in a position to give me a hard time.

"No doubt, you're dying to tell me."

She nods, looking me up and down thoughtfully. "Yeah, well, I realize you were just putting on a front. Tell me, was that car a rental? Is that why you freaked out the way you did?"

How the hell does this woman do it? Every single time she opens her mouth, she manages to annoy the fuck out of me again. "No, it's not a rental."

"Oh. I see. Then it's something you bought—or somebody bought for you—when times were better. When you had a little more security. Now? You're just a regular person who's desperate for the chance to make some cash. Pretty pathetic for somebody who insults another person for having a crappy car."

All right, I shouldn't have been so nasty and judgmental about her car. It was only because she pissed me off by laughing at the damage to my car. Still, she's right—I'm not in any place to judge. Does that stop me from squinting down at her and making things worse? No. "And yet, I still drive a better car than you."

Her eyes widen ever so slightly with hurt before she turns her back on me.

Why do I feel like a jerk? Like I just made a big mistake?

I don't have time to think about it because another snooty looking PA, a woman, comes out and walks down the length of the line. "All right, people, we'll be taking you in groups of twenty for the audience to look you over."

"Audience?" several people mutter, looking at each other.

The listing said nothing about being in front of a live audience. That doesn't bother me—if I'm going to make it on the show, there will be a lot more people watching. Might as well get used to it now.

"We didn't expect so many of you, so let me tell you how this interview is going to work," she continued, her eyes flicking towards me and lingering for a couple of seconds on me.

I sense my advantage and smile back.

She turns away with a smile. There's promise there.

Dakota is shaking her head in disgust.

This distracts me and I turn to her. *"What?"* I mouth.

"To think you called me a bimbo. What are you? Flirting with

16

the staff to get some special attention? Ugh, you make me sick."

I open my mouth to say something equally rude and the PA says, "Can I have your attention please?"

The long line of people go dead silent as everybody waits to hear what she is going to announce.

"As the ad stipulated, there's a chance to make one million dollars as a result of winning the game. You read that correctly," she pauses. "But there's no way we'll make winning a million bucks easy on you."

CHAPTER 4

TRENT

There are sighs and grumbles all down the line.

"Of course not," Dakota mutters in front of me.

"If you are chosen to be a contestant on the show, you will receive text messages which contain instructions for stunts that the audience has voted for you to perform. These stunts will all be outrageous—this is the nature of the game. If any of you believe this is not the game for you, now is the moment to walk out." She stops and pauses.

Not one person leaves the line.

"Good. If you have the courage to perform a stunt, a predetermined sum of money will be added to your overall total, and you'll be sent to the next level of the game. With every level you go up, the amount of money you can win increases. If you do not perform a stunt or fail, however, you will forfeit all of your past earnings and be kicked out of the game."

"What kind of stunts will we be asked to do?" someone down the line asks.

"What happens if we get in trouble for the stunts?" another asks.

"If I end up in jail, are you gonna bail me out?" a woman asks aggressively.

All good questions, none of which the PA answers. She just raises her hand for silence. "That kind of information will only be divulged if you are chosen to be a contestant."

Probably a liability issue, I guess. They're not allowed to make any promises. And I'd go so far as to guess that no, the show's producers would not want to be held accountable for the repercussions of the stunts. After all, if a contestant doesn't feel comfortable, or if they feel a stunt will result in harm or jail time, they shouldn't do it. That's how the producers will wash their hands of the entire situation. It's almost insulting.

But I need the money.

"Over the course of the game, the number of players will of course, dwindle," she continues. "Until only one remains standing. That player will be the winner who will take home the million dollars."

A cheer rises from the crowd and fills the hallway.

I'm not cheering. There's nothing to cheer about and I'm too focused to cheer. Let the rest of them act like idiots. I'm here to win.

I notice I'm not the only one too focused to applaud.

Little blondie who needs to take driving lessons is also silent, her brow creases in a frown. She's probably thinking of the nature of the outrageous stunts.

It's a shame she's such a raging bitch, or else I'd ask what she thinks of all this. I'm sure she has a good reason for being here. As crass as she comes off, there's still a touch of class to her. She's gorgeous, but she didn't dress like a whore to get the audience's attention. I can't help but feel a grudging sense of respect for her. But only because of that.

"All right. Let's take the first twenty."

The line starts to move as the first group of people are let into the studio. There's a buzz of excitement, intrigue, and a hell of a lot of nervous tension. I have steel nerves and even I'm feeling a little edgy. The thought of performing outrageous stunts in front of a live audience broadcast across the country isn't something I cherish. I'm fairly sure I'll want to leave this experience off my resume, even when I win the million. And I do intend to win. My palms are a little clammy, but I remind myself that this is the sort of energy I feed upon. It strengthens me and solidifies my resolve.

I steal a glance at Dakota. I wonder what she's thinking, still standing in front of me and keeping to herself the way I am. She barely flinched all throughout the description of what we would have to do. She's pretty determined. It's a shame she won't win, if she even gets the chance to play.

After a few minutes, the line moves again. And again. It's not taking long for the audience to decide whether they like their potential contestants. How are they choosing them? At random? What happens when they reach a limit? It's not like they can call people back in. I guess somebody knows what they're doing, but it all seems a little random to me.

Time passes and we keep moving.

Soon, I can see the door and people going through it as each new group is called in. There's no chance to get a feeling for what's going on in there because nobody comes out of the door as the assistants are obviously shuffling people out of another door. The walls must be pretty tightly soundproofed too, since I hear nothing coming from in there.

Within two hours, it's our turn. *Time to shine, Trent.* We're guided into the studio and led through a series of doors. As we are taken around a corner, I start to hear people, shuffling, coughing, clearing their throats, and murmuring among themselves. It sounds like a fairly big audience. I plaster on my brightest smile as we take another corner, and step onto a brightly lit set.

The audience applauds, but without much enthusiasm. They've been at this all morning. The man in the button-down shirt and khakis who is holding a microphone and wearing a smile that looks like it was painted on by the makeup crew doesn't look tired, though. He's fucking radiant. Grinning and looking excited to see us so jazzed up. I'm thinking maybe, there's a caffeine IV somewhere that he keeps taking hits off.

"All right, ladies and gentlemen! You are our last group of the day! I know our audience is tired and I'm sure you are, so let's get right down to it!"

The set is bare but for a nest of cream sofas and a long coffee table. This must be where the host will hold live interviews with the contestants. A crew member directs us, and we start to form two lines in front of the audience. The lights are in our faces and it is impossible to make theirs out.

Dakota stands next to me, I have to jerk my chin and point to motion for her to move down a little so there's room for me. She wants to edge me out. Probably knows I'll win and doesn't want me in the running. When she doesn't move, I move her by stepping onto the low stage and using my larger body to force her into taking a few steps to her left.

She almost falls.

A few members of the audience notice this and laugh.

She doesn't laugh, of course. Her hazel eyes burn with fury as she glares up at me and very deliberately stamps on my foot.

I wince but hold back any stronger reaction than that. There are more laughs from the audience. God, it really doesn't take much to entertain people these days.

Still grinning like a Cheshire cat, the host turns to face all of us. "My name is Chip Douglas."

"No, it isn't," Dakota mutters to herself.

I secretly agree. Nobody's name is Chip.

"And I'm sure one of the production assistants has already explained the rules of the game. The audience has already picked nineteen other teams to participate—all we need is a team from this group!" He encourages the audience to cheer at this, while those of us on the set look at each other in surprise.

"Team?" one of the others asks.

"Yes, a team. Two people. We're looking for two people with the right...chemistry." Chip's smile seems a little more demonic all the time. He knows this is a surprise to all of us and he is enjoying himself thoroughly. "Sorry. Did they not tell you about that part?"

"You know they didn't, because you probably got the same response from the other teams," Dakota pipes up.

"So it's not just me you're rude to," I murmur.

"Listen, you smug ass," she mutters under her breath. "I'm not here to argue with you."

"No. You're here to argue with the guy who's hosting the show," I hiss.

Chip walks over to us. "Are you two a couple?" he asks, winking at the audience.

They chuckle knowingly, and it's enough to make my skin crawl. "Definitely not," I say, shaking my head. "We're *complete* strangers."

"He stole my space in the parking lot," she announces vindictively.

"No, I damn well didn't. She doesn't know how to drive."

"He needs glasses. I was already in there well before him."

"She needs a good spanking," I finish with clenched teeth. At that moment, I would have liked nothing better than to have her splayed on my lap and my palm striking her sassy ass.

I hear her gasp with shock.

The crowd howls with laughter.

"Ouch," Chip replies, tugging at his shirt collar with one finger. "It's getting a little heated in here, folks. I think these two need to hug it out."

"I don't think so," we reply in unison.

The audience goes wild with laughter.

I feel a flush creeping along my neck, threatening to reach my face. It's one thing to be in front of hundreds of people but quite another to hear them laughing at me.

Chip turns to the audience with another wink. "I don't know about you folks, but I think I see the start of a beautiful friendship here. Or at least, a working relationship. What do you think?"

"Yes!" They cheer, whistle, and stomp their feet.

"I don't believe this," Dakota mutters over their cheers.

I have no response, because I don't believe it either.

"What's your name?" he asks her, pointing his microphone in her direction.

"Dakota," she says with a quiver in her voice. Yes, it's one thing to pretend to be brave but another to know you're in the hot seat.

"And you, big guy?" Chip smiles at me, sounding like we're old friends instead of strangers. His eyes are too green to be real, his skin too tan to be natural.

"Trent," I reply.

"Dakota and Trent," he shouts in the microphone. He turns towards the audience his face glowing. "I like the sound of that, don't you?" he says persuasively to the room of people sitting in front of us.

There's an earpiece in one of his ears and I'm sure somebody watching from somewhere in the building is feeding him instructions. They like us together. They want him to get the audience to choose us as the last team.

I want nothing less in the world than to work with her—except not winning the money. Getting that million is more important to me than anything, even my pride. Or else I wouldn't be auditioning for a damned game show in the first place. I'm going to have to swallow my pride just one more time if I'm going to get what I showed up for.

"Audience, pick up your voting devices and press 'One' if you want to see Dakota and Trent team up, or 'Two' if you think we should pick another team." Chip smiles at us with the look of a man who knows what's coming.

I know what's coming, too. I can feel it. Because my luck is just that shitty today.

We look up at the screen behind us. Sure enough, the vote's unanimous. We're a team.

"Thank you for coming," Chip says to the other eighteen who came in with us. I feel sorry for them for a second—they waited all that time and nobody paid attention to them. But I feel worse for myself, truth be told, because I'm stuck with the most obnoxious person I've ever met.

Hatred just about radiates from her as she glowers up at me.

The audience, meanwhile, eats it up with a spoon.

"Well, you two. It looks like you're going to round out our teams for this season of the show! How do you feel?" He shoves the microphone in my face, still wearing that outrageous grin.

I wonder if he just had Botox or something and his face is

semi-frozen that way. "Excellent." I look down at Dakota, who glowers up at me. "It'll be a good competition."

"I'm sure it will," Chip agrees—and judging by their applause, so does the audience. "One of the assistants will take down your personal information just outside this studio. You'll get your first text message tomorrow, containing instructions for your first stunt."

I'm in a sort of daze as a crew member ushers us to a door, then steers us in the direction of a production assistant who takes down our names and phone numbers. We sign waivers releasing the production company from liability—saw that one coming—and are free to go.

It's like touching back down after getting sucked up into a tornado. The two of us walk to the elevator and take it down to the ground floor, then walk out to the parking lot without saying a word. What is there to say? I fully intend to win the game, which means I'll eventually have to beat her—I guess they'll turn us on each other once we're the last team standing.

I glance at her as I open the car door. She's visibly shaken. For the briefest of moments, I feel sorry for her. She doesn't really want to do this. Not because she's scared—I get the feeling she can handle herself—but because she simply doesn't like the idea. Neither do I, really, but this is my last option. Maybe it's her last option too.

"See you tomorrow," I call out.

She shoots me a look. "So long as it's not in the parking lot."

"Yeah." I can't help but smile as I slide behind the steering wheel and pull out of my spot.

CHAPTER 5

DAKOTA

The reality of what just happened doesn't fully hit me until I park in front of my house. I'm sitting behind the wheel shaking, hands gripping the vinyl so tight my knuckles look bone white.

I wanted to get on the show. I planned to, but I guess I didn't really expect to. *A million dollars.* I can't even imagine that much money. Not that I need to. I know exactly what I would do with it. Even so, the thought that it could be mine is overwhelming. I need a minute to process before I get out of the car.

A minute is all I have before I need to get inside. The house is one of the few assets Mom owns free and clear. The car is another one—it used to be hers, but she can't drive anymore so she lets me use it. Not that it's worth much. If it were, I would sell it just to have the money and take the bus to work every day. It would take another hour to get there and back, but if it meant paying off just one more bill…

"Mom? I'm home." I slide out of my shoes the moment I step

foot inside the front door. She's watching her game shows, as always. I wonder what she'd think if she knew, I just landed a spot in one of them? Well, she'll never know. She doesn't watch reality TV or any of the interactive game shows currently out there. Hates them. The classics are much more her speed. That's how I know I'll be safe and she'll never know the lengths I went to in order to pay for her treatment. *The Price is Right* blares from the TV across from the bed I set up in the living room.

"It's not the same since Bob Barker left the show," she murmurs, shaking her head.

Like I haven't heard that comment at least once a week since she got sick and TV became her life. I settle down in the easy chair next to the bed and pat her hand. "I know. He was before my time. Hasn't he been off the show for years and years?"

"Don't remind me." She offers me a weak smile. "I don't need to remember how old I am."

"Oh, stop it. I wouldn't even call you middle-aged."

"I feel a lot older." Her smile fades.

"I know."

And another one of those awkward silences falls over us. The only sound in the room is the screaming of a contestant who just won a car. We watch as the picture on the TV fades to black and a commercial starts.

"How was your interview?" she asks.

I give her the widest smile I can call up. "Great. I got the position."

"You did? Oh, that's wonderful news! I needed something to cheer me up today…you should've told me right away."

I run my hand over her forehead. No fever. "What's wrong that you needed something to cheer you up?"

She grimaces. "Nothing out of the ordinary."

"You know it's going to get better. Right? It will, once we get you that treatment."

"That treatment," she murmurs, waving one weak hand. "It's nothing but a fantasy. We can't pay for it."

"Don't lose hope, Mom. I have a good feeling about this. Now that I've got this job I think there is a chance that we're going to be able to afford the treatment." I hate lying to her, and I've never been any good at it. She's always been able to spot a lie too, but something about having cancer has weakened her inner detector. She believes I have a new job.

She doesn't believe it'll be enough, though. "Do you know how much that sort of therapy costs? Yeah, they have all these commercials for special treatment centers and their high rates of success, but they don't tell you the cost. Insurance isn't going to cover even part of that."

"What did the doctor tell you last time we went in to see him? Hmm?" I pull the covers a little tighter around her thin frame, then sit on the edge of the bed with her hand in mine. It's so thin, so delicate. "He told you not to worry over things you can't control. The more you think about the money and the insurance, the worse you're going to feel. You have to keep your energy focused on healing and being well."

"You sound like a woo-woo, hippy-dippy fruitcake," she murmurs, but there is a cheeky smile on her face.

"Yeah, well, maybe I am right now. Because I do believe this is going to turn out alright. They caught it early enough that you should be able to get well and go into remission—but you need this treatment and I'm going to make sure you get it."

She wants to believe. I can feel it in the way her fingers tighten around mine. Even so, her eyes search my face. "What are you doing to earn this money?" she whispers.

"What?"

"What sort of position offers you enough money to pay for me to go to a fancy treatment center? You're twenty-two years old. You're a personal assistant. That's all the experience you have. What are you going to have to do for it?"

"It's nothing illegal, and it's nothing to be ashamed of," I promise her. "Just trust me a little. Okay?"

She sighs. "I want to trust you. I do. But I can't let you degrade yourself, or do anything you'll regret later. Not for me. I should be the one taking risks for you, making sacrifices for you." Tears fill her eyes.

"You don't think you've done enough for me?" I ask, reaching out to wipe away a tear that's spilled onto her cheek. She's so much thinner than she used to be and she's always been on the thin side. Her skin is so delicate. "You raised me as a single mother. You worked two jobs to keep this roof over our heads and managed to pay off the mortgage years ahead of schedule. You sat up at night with me when I had stomach bugs and the flu, and still went to work in the morning. Nobody was here to take care of you over all those years, so you took care of yourself and me." It was my turn to cry.

"Why wouldn't I do this for you? It's my chance to pay you back in some small way for everything you've done."

"I don't want you to pay me back."

"Too bad. I'm going to anyway. So, you'd better sit back and get used to it. Okay?"

She shakes her head but there's a resigned sort of admiration in her eyes. She knows there's nothing she can do about me stepping up the way I am. She might even be proud of me, though it's hurting her to feel like a burden. I'm doing everything I can to make sure she never feels that way, but I can't seem to change her stubborn mind. I guess we're both pretty stubborn.

Her eyes slide shut. "I'm so tired." She's always tired in the days, immediately after chemo.

"You get some sleep, then." I turn the TV down to a low rumble...she doesn't like sleeping without any noise in the background, something that she picked up when she got sick. Maybe it's fear of slipping into eternal silence. I tuck her in more securely. "I'll be in the kitchen if you wake up and need anything."

"Alight." She's already breathing softly and evenly by the time I leave her side.

CHAPTER 6

DAKOTA

When she's asleep, I can let down my guard a little. I feel myself crumbling slowly as I sink into a chair at the kitchen table. How many times have I sat here over the years? Same table too. Birthday cakes, Christmas cookies, and late-night heart-to-hearts. Saturday morning pancakes.

I miss those days.

I miss being a little girl, of not having to worry about where the money is coming from, or how fast Mom's body is deteriorating. She's fading before my very eyes and all I want to do is hold onto her, clutch her to me, order her to stay around and get better.

I can't imagine losing her. Not yet. She's too young. She ought to be out there, enjoying life. She hasn't even seen her forty-fifth birthday. There's still so much for her to explore and do, then maybe, finally, find the true love she's always dreamed about and never found.

Instead, she's lying in a bed in the living room day after day, watching reruns of game shows.

A gentle tap on the back door shakes me out of my depressed thoughts. I barely have time to raise my head from my palms before Jenny steps into the kitchen. She knows by now that she doesn't have to wait for permission to come in.

"Oh, no," she says, sitting across from me with a look of anguish. "I guess it didn't go well."

"Actually, it went more than well. I got on the show."

"You did?" Her face lights up. "That's fantastic!"

"Yeah. I guess." I sit back in my chair, chewing on my lip. "Now I just have to win. But what if I don't? This is my last chance to get the money together. I mean, sitting here like this, thinking about it... How did I ever think this was a solid idea? It's a total shot in the dark."

"Listen." She leans over the table. "You've got a real shot at this. As good a shot as anybody else they chose."

"But what if the audience gives me something I just can't bring myself to do?"

"They're not allowed to ask you to do anything that'll get you into serious trouble." She pauses. "Are they?"

"I have no idea. I mean, they can't make it too easy, or else nobody would win. The game would just go on and on without anybody dropping out."

"Hmm. That's true."

"And there are twenty teams, so they're going to need to weed out the duds pretty quickly."

"Wait. Teams? You're on a team? I thought it was just one person working alone."

My blood starts to simmer at the thought of him. The smug bastard. "No. Unfortunately, I have a teammate, and he's the worst." I give her the brief rundown of our meeting, if it can even be called that. More like a showdown.

She sits back, arms folded, a smirk touching her lips. "Lemme get this straight. He's hotter than chili flavored Cheetos, probably has, at least, a little money, and the two of you have to spend time doing crazy things together. Am I hitting all the main points of this story?"

"Yes." I roll my eyes with a sigh. We've been friends our entire lives, so I know where she's going with this.

Her gray eyes narrow. "Tell me again what the big problem is?"

"The big problem is, he's a total jerk."

She makes a disbelieving face.

"No, really," I whisper, glancing over my shoulder into the living room to make sure I don't wake Mom. "The man is a male version of a bimbo. I could carve a better personality out of a potato."

She giggles.

"It's all right for you. You don't have to deal with his arrogant ass. The only consolation will be seeing his face when I beat him somehow, once we're the only team left standing. I pray I can do it."

"You'll find a way. I know you will. Hell, if you learn enough about him and the way he thinks while you're working together, you might be able to figure out how to beat him in the end."

"Hmm. That's a good point." I smile at her. "This is why I keep you around. You're smarter than I am."

"Nah. Just more devious." We both giggle softly for fear of disturbing Mom.

"Thanks for looking in on her today," I add as I get up to fix a glass of iced tea for both of us.

"You thank me everyday, and I always tell you not to worry about it."

"But I'm still going to thank you. I mean, you have other things to do."

"Like what? Sleeping? Because that's usually what I do if I'm not working." She takes the iced tea and sips it with a thoughtful look on her face. "And you're changing the subject, by the way."

Damn it. She knows me too well. "What do you mean?" I ask as I sit back down with what I hope is an innocent look on my face, but she sees straight through me.

"We were talking about Mr. Hottie and you totally took a left turn. Why are you avoiding talking about him? He's gonna be your teammate. You'd better get used to him."

"I don't think I've ever taken such an instant dislike to anyone before," I mutter, shaking my head. "He's an awful human being. I might have to really watch him. He may be one of those charming psychopaths. The heartless way he kicked my purse of out of that elevator."

"Did you just call him charming?"

I jerk my head. "I didn't."

"Yes, you did. You said he may be one of those charming psychopaths."

I frown. "I didn't mean to say that. It was slip of the tongue. He is not charming at all. Every time he opens his mouth, I want to toss a Xanax into it."

"He was only reacting," she says, wrinkling her nose. "Quite frankly, I don't think anybody's gonna be kind and sweet when they just got dinged by another driver. And he was probably stressed over the audition, just like you were."

"Whose side are you on?"

"I didn't know I had to pick a side," she murmurs with a grin.

I widen my eyes at her.

"Oh well, yours, I guess."

"Then maybe you should stop making me feel bad about hating him."

"I'm not trying to make you feel bad…and I don't think you hate him."

"You don't know what you're talking about. Believe me, if you had been there, you would understand. I can't put it into words, but he made me feel awful. I wanted to strangle him or at least kick him in the balls."

"Oh, a kick in the balls? It sounds like the beginning of a delicious love affair to me."

I roll my eyes. "You tend bar for a living. Don't measure this by the random hookups you see every night."

She laughs. "Which reminds me, I wanted to tell you about the two I served last night. They were obviously on a first date, and it was clearly through a dating app because neither of them recognized the other one from their profile pics. The girl actually kept mentioning how different the guy looked and kept asking him questions to make sure he was the same guy she had been talking to."

I smile and she launches into one of her stories of the sad, bizarre encounters she watches during every shift. I let her story take me out of my head for a little while. The first text comes in tomorrow, and I'll have more than enough time to worry about what's coming to me when it arrives. Until then, a glass of iced tea and a little girl talk with my best friend is exactly what the doctor ordered.

Even so, I can't keep from hearing the sound of Mom's light, shallow breathing coming from behind me.

CHAPTER 7

TRENT

I stand in the middle of my renovated factory and experience a sense of real pride. This place is going to look amazing one day. I just know it. The space alone is incredible. There's so much character in a building like this. A whole different class than some drywall-and-concrete monstrosity. The exposed brick and original wide-plank flooring are a great touch too. I walk over to the tall, wide windows and look out at the majestic view of the river, and the Ben Franklin Bridge. It's breathtakingly beautiful. I want my employees to come to work every day feeling like they're part of something with soul.

Of course, I need employees first. But at least, I have the office space settled.

I loosen my tie and slide out of my jacket before sitting at my desk. It's only lunch time, but it feels like it has been a long day. No doubt, there'll be longer days if I plan to pull off winning this game show, but that's cool with me. I'm used to hard work. Anybody who's ever tried to get a business off the ground knows what eighteen hours days are all about.

I pull up my email and pop open an energy drink at the same time, ready to dive in and really start the work day. Taking the morning off to go to that audition was a risky move, one which I would have regretted if I hadn't made it.

But I did make it.

And I'm going to go all the way to the end. I'm going to turn this business into what I've been dreaming of for the last three years, ever since I had a big idea in my dorm room at the end of senior year.

A lot has changed since then. I'm not a fresh-faced college kid anymore or living off my parents. Life sure was a lot easier when you didn't have to earn your own money, or pay bills. When I look back on how busy I thought I was throughout college, I can't help but laugh at myself. Studying and playing sports. Wow, what a tough life I had. Spoiled brat. I wish I could go back and give that old version of me a solid punch in the jaw sometimes.

If I could, I'd tell him to get a clue, too.

I'd warn him against the pitfalls I've already fallen into, only three years in. I'd tell him to take his time trusting people, to not let supposed friends fool him into thinking they'd make good business partners. I'd advise him to set aside more than he thinks is necessary for the tax man because there's nothing like finding out money is owed at the end of the financial year, money that's already been earmarked for other things. I learned that the hard way.

Eric comes in carrying a bag from a sandwich shop on the corner. "Dude, I didn't expect you back so soon," he says, putting the bag on his desk and sliding into his chair.

It's an open floor plan, so I can see him from where I am, halfway across the room. "Yeah, I came back about twenty minutes ago." I keep my eyes on my monitor and pretend nothing's up, just to screw with him for a little bit.

"So?"

I can see he's trying to be casual, but he's itching to know. "So what?" I ask with a yawn.

"Did you make it or not?"

I have to take pity on the guy. He doesn't have the same stake in the company as I do, but he does have a vested interest in whether or not we succeed. I promised him a twenty-five percent share of the business if we get it off the ground. And he would deserve it too, as he's the most loyal, hardworking person I've found so far.

I look at him expressionlessly to drag out the suspense a little longer.

"Well?" he prompts.

"Yeah. I made it," I shout with a grin.

"Shut the fuck up! You seriously did?" He jumps out of his chair and pumps his fist.

"What? You doubted me?" I chuckle.

"No offense, man. I've seen you pull some crazy shit before, all in the name of getting this business off the ground, but this is in a class by itself. Too many variables in play at once."

I wave it off. "Whatever. I had it in the bag the second I walked in."

"When do you start?"

"Tomorrow."

He winces. "Wow. They don't even give you any time to get your life in order before you have to start doing the stunts?"

"Right," I nod. "Hey—the sooner we start, the sooner the money's in the bank and we can really get this thing rolling." Everything I've worked for in the last three years comes down to this. Nothing less than my entire life, really. If this fails, I'll have to start from scratch. Every cent I've earned, raised, or borrowed is at stake. Everything in my life.

"You think you'll win it?" he asks before taking a bite of what smells like an Italian hoagie with extra onions.

I can't help but scowl. "First, you tell me you doubted that I'd make the show. Now you're doubting that I'll take home the prize. Have some confidence, man."

"Hey, the tech world has its ups and downs and massive change can occur overnight—but that's still not as crazy as this show is gonna be for you."

"Is that your idea of a pep talk? Because it's not all that inspiring. You need to watch some sports movies and figure out where you're going wrong."

He laughs and shrugs off my sarcasm. "All I'm saying is…it's gonna be intense."

One of the many reasons we work so well together is he lets things roll off his back, while I'm way too serious. "Like the last three years haven't been intense. Believe me, man, I get where you're coming from, but I have it under control. You don't need to worry about a thing." I chuckle darkly. "Besides, I'm fairly sure there's only one person I have to worry about."

"Who?"

"My teammate."

His eyebrows shoot up. "Teammate?"

"Yeah. Her name's Dakota."

"Oh. Dakota, huh?"

I've known him long enough to know exactly where his mind is going. I hold up both hands, laughing. "It's not like that. Believe me. She's not my type."

"Your type is no type."

"There's no time for women." For the last few years, I've been throwing all my time and energy into developing our product, and building a business around manufacturing it.

"You could find the time if you wanted to," he says chewing slowly.

"Maybe I don't want to, then." I have no intention of sacrificing even a piece of my dream just because I need to get my dick wet on the regular. There are always women willing for a quick hookup, I've never had a problem with that, but there's no time for anything more.

Eric knows this, but still feels the need to bust my balls over it every now and again. "Okay, okay. So what happens when you two win? Do you split the prize with her?"

I like that he used the word 'when'. "I'm guessing she's the competition after that," I muse, tapping my fingers on my desk. "I'll take her out. No worries about that. The money is as good as ours."

He smiles before becoming serious. "Listen. I know I give

you a lot of shit, but I wanna let you know this means alot to me. Thanks for doing this for us."

"Hey…like I told you from day one. I'm all-in. This has been my dream for too long to let a little thing like lack of capital end it."

His phone rings and he answers. "Hello Sukie," he says cheerfully while grimacing at me.

Sukie is an aspartame drinking bitch, who unfortunately is also our only potential investor. We've been courting her for three months. She has sadistic tendencies. She knows we have a solid business plan and we're going to make her a lot of money, but she just likes to see how many hoops she can get us to jump through first. I'd really like to tell her to take a running jump, but I know I should keep her on the hook, just in case things fall through with the show. I give him the thumbs-up.

He flashes me one in return before diving into his conversation.

Don't put all your eggs in one basket, something my father used to say to me. It was one of his favorite sayings, and it's something I remind myself of every time I get too excited about the game show. That's why we're still jumping through Sukie's mean little hoops and hoping she comes through on her promises. I won't let my dream die. I can't. If something goes wrong and I don't win the show, I still have a backup plan.

But I will win.

I turn my chair away from Eric and look out of the window. It's easier to think when I can look out over the river. I'll do everything in my power to make that money mine. If I freak out over a stunt, I'll just remember everyday of these lean years, eating nothing but ramen or cereal for days on end, just to afford rent while I peddled my designs around to potential buyers. I decided to produce it myself, when none of the buyers were willing to let me have a say in production. I might have been a little too hasty then, but I was still cocky enough to believe nobody knew my product better than I did. The clock is ticking and I still haven't proven myself right.

I have to win.

I think of Dakota. She's got a nasty temper and a hell of a foul mouth to match, but I can tell she's probably never done anything crazy in her whole life. It's one thing to tell yourself you would do something for money, but another to actually go through with it, especially knowing millions of people are going to see the footage. It'll be nerve-wracking and if she's not completely committed, we're dead in the water. I'll have to convince her to go through with the stunts.

So…they were looking for a couple with the right chemistry. I try to imagine the sort of things the audience will want from us. An image of Dakota naked and bouncing on my dick, with those gorgeous breasts free, flashes into my mind.

Just like that, I'm hard as a rock.

Fuck, how long has it even been since I got laid? I actually can't remember. It's been that busy lately. My inbox is chock full of emails again. I had just finished answering messages before I left for the audition this morning. It's nonstop—inquiry replies, parts manufacturers offering quotes, latest updates from our marketing firm. No wonder I've got an erection just thinking about a woman.

I lean back against my chair. A spring is broken in the seat and it needs to be replaced, but I'm not going to spend good money on making myself comfortable. I shift slightly and my thoughts return to Dakota. No, I wouldn't mind at all if the audience chose a sexy stunt for us to pull. Making out in public, or maybe something even more risky. I could definitely live with an excuse.

I stop myself before my fantasy goes too far.

Fucking chill out, Trent.

She's already in my head. What would she think if she knew I was sitting here, thinking about her, steadily getting harder every time I picture her in my head? Before my erection gets any more obvious, I need to stop thinking about her. It's not only the idea of Eric busting my balls for the rest of my life either. It's the danger of getting too close to her and losing focus. I can't fall into the trap of seeing her as a hot girl. The last thing I want to do is start thinking with my dick. When the time comes, I'm going to have to do whatever it takes to win the money.

"Yo, man. You listening?"

"Hmm?" I barely turn my head in Eric's direction.

"Sukie wants dinner tonight. You in?"

I consider it, then shake my head. "No, I can't. You go."

"What?" His jaw drops. "You're actually gonna let me go on my own?"

"She likes you better than me, anyway. She finds you more approachable." I grin.

"No, she doesn't."

"I've seen her eyes light up."

"She's, like, a hundred years old," he groans, dropping his chin in his hand and looking miserable.

"Yeah, but you know what they say about older women. They know tricks women our age haven't even heard of yet."

His face flushes dark red. "You don't actually think I would sleep with her, do you?"

"Well…" I shrug, trying not to laugh.

"You're sick, man. Sick. Ugh." He shudders.

"You're making too big a deal of this," I joke. "I think you've already thought about it, or you wouldn't keep trying to convince me I'm wrong."

His mouth falls open again. "I'm trying to convince you that you're wrong because you seriously just grossed me out."

"Whatever, man. I wouldn't blame you if you went for it. She's hot for an older woman."

"She's not!" he sputters, shaking his head, and shuddering again.

"She's got that classy thing going on, you know?"

"So does my mom!" he argues.

It's too much fun, having the chance to bust his balls for once. "So what? Your mom is hot too."

"I'm gonna straight-up kill you."

"Whatever. I'm just saying, if she was interested in taking things back to her penthouse…" I raise my eyebrows and let the thought trail off while he fumes.

"I would do just about anything for this company you're trying to get off the ground, but I'll be damned if I'm gonna sleep with a woman three times my age, just to get the money."

"Suit yourself." I grin, turning back to the window. I'm not serious and he knows it—though it wouldn't be the worst thing in the world if he convinced her to invest…

CHAPTER 8

DAKOTA

My hands won't stop shaking. I wipe them down my jeans nervously. I don't want to show up on camera with shaking hands. Are there cameras set up around me? There could be, for all I know. I'm not sure how the show works, exactly, but there's got to be a way for the audience to see what we're doing.

I look up at the department store. I don't remember when it was a John Wanamaker's, but Mom does. They still do the Christmas light show here every year, and we've gone every year even though it hasn't changed a bit in all this time. We would then go for lunch and do some shopping together. It's something I've looked forward to every year.

We won't go this year.

My heart hurts a little when I think about that. So much is changing so quickly. But next year...next year, we'll go, because Mom will be alright by then and she'll be able to do simple things like Christmas shopping.

The thought of her illness and the treatment she needs gives me strength and courage. I'm going to need all the courage I can get, once it's time to get the stunt started.

And it would be, if Trent would ever show up. I swear to God, if he chickens out on me…

He shows up before I get the chance to complete my thought. "What took you so long?" I ask, telling myself not to notice how utterly, utterly gorgeous he looks in a tailored black shirt and jeans that seem to strain around his thick, muscular thighs. I shouldn't be paying attention to his thighs. Or his eyes as he slides his sunglasses off.

"Sorry," he says. "Some of us have to deal with a little thing called traffic."

"Oh, that's cute. Because there's no such thing as traffic, where I come from." I look around, eyes darting back and forth. People are turning their heads to look at him. At that moment, I realize that I'm really lucky they paired me off with him, because it was obvious he was going to be picked. Who's not going to watch him? "They're probably watching us right now."

"Yeah. Probably." He grins. "And they probably love it."

"Yeah, well…" I can't say what I want to say. I can't call them a bunch of vultures who get off on watching other people suffer and make fools of themselves. Talk about a sure-fire way to get kicked off the show. I look down at my phone, clutched in my palm. "Did your text say anything other than to be here at this time?" I ask.

"Nope."

"Terrific." I feel like a doofus standing around with him. "Are we maybe supposed to check in and announce that we're here?"

"Why are you asking me these things like I'm gonna know the answers?"

He sounds irritated and I whirl my head around to look at him. We stare at each other for a beat, and it takes everything I have in me not to kick him in the balls. "Why are you in such a crabby mood today? Somebody scratch your precious car again?"

"I'm riding my motorcycle today."

Yeah, because that doesn't make him sound like even more of a jerk? The guy's got a nice car and a motorcycle, and he acted like I just killed his dog when I barely scratched the car. Spoiled baby. "Oh. Well. Very masculine. Congratulations on that."

He winces and that feels good, somehow.

Our phones ding at the same time.

"Saved by the bell," he mutters as he pulls up the text.

So do I. And my jaw hits the ground, or just about.

'*Congratulations. You have made it to the destination of your first stunt. Enter the store, but do not come out wearing the clothes in which you went inside in. You are not allowed to buy any of the merchandise. You have fifteen minutes to complete your stunt. The clock starts as soon as you finish reading this text,*' I read, as I feel myself break out in a cold sweat.

I look up at him and he is staring at me with a frown. Just like that, we're on the same page. And we're both gobsmacked.

"They don't come right out and say it, probably for legal reasons, but they want us to steal, don't they?" I whisper, horrified.

"I guess so." He looks inside the building.

My gaze follows his. It is full of people, but worse, a security guard goes through the door. My stomach feels like somebody poured concrete in it. "I'm not doing this. I can't get arrested." I start hyperventilating. "I'm not a thief. They can't force us to break the law like this." I glance up at him, trying to gauge his feelings.

He nods. "I know. Maybe we can get away with it somehow, and not get in trouble."

"Are you kidding? The clothes in these stores have tags on them. Security tags. As soon as we walk past the sensors, we're caught. I'm not going to prison." My voice is high and squeaky. There is no way I'm going to steal.

"How fast can you run?" he asks, with a wink.

"Can you be serious?" I snap, losing my fear in my anger.

"I was being serious."

"You're crazy. I'm not doing it." I dance from one foot to the other and wonder if the audience will think it's funny when I pee my pants, because that's pretty much what I feel like I'm about to do. I can already see myself getting handcuffed and arrested for stealing an outfit I don't even need. A thought suddenly occurs to me. "What about underwear? Are we supposed to steal that as well?"

"I guess so."

"Are you okay with us being known as underwear thieves?"

"I don't give a fuck what I'm known as. I just want us to complete the stunt."

"Millions of people are going to see us stealing from a department store. I'll never going to get another job in my life. This is—"

"So you're just going to give up?" he cuts in coldly.

It's like a bucket of freezing water chucked in my face. I lose my hysteria instantly. I take a deep breath. "No."

"Well, then stop wasting time. Let's get in there, and find a way to complete the stunt inside our allotted time." He takes my hand.

I've never felt such a strong manly clasp before, but I'm too busy being scared out of my wits to pull away.

"Come on. Let's eat the frog."

"What does that even mean?" I grumble as he pulls me through the doors.

"It means get the hard stuff over with first."

"This is all hard stuff, Confucius," I mutter as I jerk my hand away from his.

We're standing in the main concourse while three floors of

departments loom above us. We both look up at the marble columns and brass railings.

"Shit," he whispers.

I can hear panic in his voice for the first time. So maybe he's human, after all. But that's not going to help us. "Where do we start, do you think?" I ask, glancing around.

"Well, first thing...let's try to stop acting like shoplifters." He takes my hand again, this time, gripping it so tight I can't pull away. He leads me to the escalator. "Just play it cool. We're here looking for clothes for an event. I don't care what. Make something up in your head to give you a story, something you'll believe."

"Your funeral?" I mutter under my breath.

"Or yours," he mutters back.

"Is a spangly red dress appropriate for a funeral?"

"Sure, you can wear a spangly red dress to my funeral, Blondie," he murmurs. "Whatever will give you something to focus on while we're walking around. If you keep telling yourself you're going to steal, you're going to act shady and suspicious."

That much, I could believe. "Okay, I'll do my best." There aren't many shoppers this early in the day, and on a weekday at that. "We would have be able to blend in better on the weekend, I think. More people. I feel so exposed."

"I'm sure they think about things like this when they set these stunts up."

"Yeah. They probably do. Do you think they are filming us right now?"

He stares ahead. "Pretty sure, they are?"

This is for Mom. This is for Mom. This is for Mom. Maybe if I say it enough, I'll feel better about what I'm going to do.

The women's section comes up first, and I can barely put one foot in front of another. "What should I choose?" I mutter, looking around.

"Something close to what you're wearing," he advises, looking me up and down. "Do they even sell clothes like that anymore?"

"I swear to God."

"Sorry, sorry. Reflex."

"It's a stinking sweater and jeans, dick," I whisper as we start looking for something suitable through the casuals. "I mean, people wear sweaters and jeans all the time." I thought I looked pretty cute when I left the house.

"Not in this weather they don't, but calm down. I was just busting your balls. We need to work together. We have less than ten minutes left." He picks out a cable-knit sweater in a similar shade of cream to the one I'm wearing. "What do you think?"

"Fine, fine." I put it over my arm.

We stop in front of a wall of folded jeans. "So. Do I dare ask what size we're looking for?"

"I'll look for my own, thanks. Why don't you worry about you?" I snap hastily.

"Fine. I will." He turns to leave—then freezes in place.

"What's the matter?" I ask filled with panic again.

When he spins back around, his eyes are twinkling and he's wearing a huge grin. "Son of a bitch! We totally missed the obvious."

CHAPTER 9

DAKOTA

"What do you mean?" I ask round-eyed with curiosity.

He leans in to whisper in my ear, "There's nothing in the message about brand new clothes. Just clothes that are different from the ones we're wearing."

Oh, how I hate the little shiver that runs down my spine when the heat from his breath hit my skin. "Huh?" I can't think straight when all I can smell is his cologne.

He pulls back and looks me in the eye. "All we have to do is switch clothes, Dakota. We'll go out in clothes that we did not come into the store in."

It sinks in slowly, and I feel like dawn just broke. "Switch clothes with each other. Oh, my God. Don't let it go to your head, but that is genius!" I toss the sweater aside. "Okay. Nearest dressing room, then." We make a beeline for the changing room. It's a women's room, but there's nobody in any of the little stalls, so I think it'll be okay. I wave him in behind me and immediately lock myself in one stall while he takes another.

"Strip down," he orders.

"Thanks for making that clear," I whisper back as I pull my sweater off and toss it over the partition. Boots come next, then jeans. I can't imagine how he thinks he'll fit into them, but maybe he can think of something. I pull off my socks next and ball them up, lobbing them over as well.

"Shit. None of these fit."

I roll my eyes. "No kidding."

"You haven't given me everything yet," he points out.

"Oh. Right." I look down at my bra and panties. "You won't fit into these, either."

"I'll make something work."

"Jesus Christ. My favorite goddamn underwear and you're going to stretch it all out." I peel off the panties and unhook the bra, thanking God the entire time that I wore my best set. If I were wearing period panties, I'd kill myself. I hand it over instead of throwing it.

"Hmm. Nice."

I jump up and swipe my arm over the top of the partition, hoping to take a swipe at him. "Shut it and give me your things, please." I'm completely naked, for God's sake.

"Okay. Here you go." He even took the time to fold everything.

Compulsive, I decide. It's all huge. Even the boxer briefs.

"Huh. Men's underwear is way more comfy than women's," I observe.

"I wish I could say the same in reverse," he groans.

I can't help but giggle as I pull on his jeans. "Oh, jeez, these are falling down even with the belt cinched all the way," I complain. "Then again, the shirt will probably be a dress on me, anyway." Sure enough, it comes almost to my knees. I carry what doesn't fit. "Are you ready?" I ask, freaked out all over again. At least the shop's entrance is not too far from where we're getting dressed, but there's still the escalator to get down and the concourse to navigate. Oh, and then the street. A very crowded, very public street complete with buses, taxis, and people. Hell, what am I worried about? Millions are going to see it on their TV screens.

"I don't think I could ever possibly be ready for this," he mutters.

I bite the side of my tongue to keep from laughing too hard. "Come on. I bet you look pretty." I open my door and step out, then rap on his with the backs of my knuckles. "Come on. Let's see."

"I look ridiculous."

"And that's different from any other time?" I ask, rolling my eyes.

"Good point." The knob turns and the door opens.

I take a deep breath and get ready to laugh, but instead—I just about fall to my knees and praise Jesus because *damn*.

"They were all that fit," he says, striking a pose in nothing but my panties.

It takes me a few seconds to recover from the first rush of blood to my nether regions. How long has it been since I? "Umm—did you stuff my socks in there?" I say waving my hand in the vague direction of his package.

"No. Why?"

"Do you have an erection?"

"No."

This *no* had a meaning all of its own. Jesus what is he packing in there? My poor underwear is straining with all the man meat stuffed into it. I clear my throat. "Well...I can't say it thrills me that my panties fit you. I don't know if I should be insulted or what."

"They're really stretchy." He turns to show me the back view, and it's about the most glorious thing I've ever seen.

He's not eye candy. He's practically the enemy. Stop this.

Only I can't help it. He's so fine.

They used to be boy shorts. Now they're a bikini. I swallow hard and try to shake off the odd sensation in my belly, but it's nearly impossible.

Silence falls heavy between us.

Something flashes in his eyes.

I've seen that look before. In other men's eyes. I shake my head. What the hell am I thinking of?

"Okay, well, we'd better get going. We have four minutes to make it out of here." He gathers up the rest of my things and turns to me. He catches me staring at him.

"You ready for this?" I ask.

His grin is positively feral. "Dakota, I'm wearing women's underwear and trying to feel secure in my manhood."

"Okay." I peek outside the dressing area to the main floor. The ladies perusing casual wear are about to get a real treat.

"Alright. Let's get this over with."

We do. I step out first and lead the way with him right behind me.

"Oh my God, everybody is looking at us," I say from between clenched teeth. I can't believe this! I can't believe I'm going to walk out of here in a man's shirt and with Trent following in my panties.

I hear a gasp, followed by what sounds like somebody dropping an armload of clothes, and maybe a purse, and maybe even a small child, but I can't be sure because I'd have to look over to be sure and that would mean possibly making eye contact and I can't do that, no way. Absolutely not. I keep my eyes front and center, a smile plastered on my face.

"I bet none of these ladies expected a show today," he says cockily behind me.

I turn around and my heart flips. He's actually strutting behind me like he owns the world. "I should've known you would get off on the attention," I mutter. Silly me, thinking for even a split second that he'd be embarrassed to wear my underwear in public. Then again, why should he be? He looks like a sex god come to life. A very tall, very cut, very handsome sex god.

"You look pretty hot yourself," he says with a wicked grin.

We step on the escalator and now I can hear flat-out laughter, catcalls and whooping. My cheeks burn from it and from him calling me pretty hot. Do I look hot? This is the second time he's called me that. I hear the clicking of phone cameras coming from just about every direction and tell myself it's not time to think about flirting. "How much time do we have left?"

He looks at his watch. "Two minutes."

We start running down the escalator. "Excuse me, excuse," as we pass people who stare openly at us.

"Get out of the way!" he yells as we hit the main concourse. A security guard catches my eye. Trent must see him, too, because he grabs my hand and we both burst out onto the street, breathless and laughing.

"I can't believe we just did that!" I gasp.

"We're not finished yet!" He takes my hand and pulls me behind him at a dead run, heading for the parking lot.

Horns honk, people cheer, I even hear one woman ask Trent to marry her as we rush past.

He looks over his shoulder with a wide, brilliant smile and shouts, "Sorry, sugar tits. I'm married to her."

Whoa! That sends a weird thrill down my spine. "Did you just call that woman sugar tits?" I pant.

"I never thought I'd see the day. You're jealous," he says with a chuckle.

"You want me to ride this with no pants on?" I gape as we reach his motorcycle, which is basically the most macho piece of machinery I've ever seen.

"Here," he says handing me my clothes. "And I'll need my pants too. I don't want to be arrested for indecent exposure." His pants are all he puts on before sliding into his shoes and throwing one leg over the chrome beast. Sunlight hits his skin making it gleam as he kicks the starter and the engine's roar fills my head as he turns back to look at me. "Hop on."

A funny warmth spreads through my core when I realize I'll be plastered up against that bare back, my arms around his waist.

"Hurry before somebody comes looking for us!" he orders.

I throw one leg over the way he did and immediately, the vibration from the engine moves all through me. Between that and the contact with Trent's bare skin, I feel myself getting wet. Hungering for him.

Only the buzzing of my phone pulls me out of it. Trent reaches for his at the same time.

Congratulations Dare Me Contestant.
You have successfully
completed your first stunt.
Prize money: $10,000

"Woo hoo!" I squeeze him a little tighter than I technically need to as we pull out of the parking garage and onto the street.

CHAPTER 10

Thank God, Mom is asleep when I get home. There's no way I could explain riding up to the house on a motorcycle, holding onto a bare chested hunk, wearing a shirt that clearly isn't mine. I'm sure I couldn't explain away the color in my cheeks, either. I can feel them burning with a mixture of excitement and pride.

I'm actually proud of myself for pulling off what we just did.

I owe most of it to him, of course. If it wasn't for him being so smart, we would've ended shoplifting and knowing my luck, I would have got caught. I wonder if the other teams had to perform the same stunts. I wonder how many of them tried to shoplift. Did any get caught? It's one way to pare down the number of competing teams. If it weren't for Trent being so level-headed, my ass would probably be in a jail cell downtown right now. I never would've pulled off stealing a new outfit.

I dash upstairs to change, intensely aware of the fact that I'm still wearing his briefs under my jeans. They are soaked and I'm feeling aroused and horny. My insides feel as if they have liquefied. I wish I could slip under the covers and end this torment.

Not now.

I slip out of his underwear and for some strange reason hold it close to my cheek. Knowing him, he'll ask for them back. I blush again when I imagine my body rubbing up against his. I giggle to myself. Yes, he's a pain in the ass, but he's also…intriguing.

And hot. Very hot.

And fun. And sexy. Oh, God the way his hard body felt.

I feel more like myself once I'm in my own clothes again. I can breathe easily as I sit on the edge of my bed and reflect on the insanity my life has become. We'll get another stunt tonight. I wonder what they'll have us do this time.

I hear a sound from the baby monitor I have fixed up in my room. Mom's stirring. Good thing I came in when I did. I jog downstairs.

She jumps in surprise. "I didn't know you came in."

"I only did a few minutes ago." I bend down to kiss her forehead and immediately regret it when Mom crinkles her nose.

"You smell different," she notes, looking up at me with those sharp eyes of hers.

"Probably because I just spent part of the morning with a man, but not the way you think I did," I add hastily. I haven't done anything to be ashamed of. Not yet. I would've shoplifted if Trent hadn't thought fast though.

"Expensive cologne," she murmurs with a sly smile. "Must be quite a man."

"He's not a big deal," I tell her with a shrug. "I mean, he obviously thinks he is, but he isn't."

"Obviously?"

"You know what I mean. He's handsome, but he knows he's handsome. It's annoying."

"Annoying?"

"Are you a parrot now?" I ask with a smile.

"You're a little edgy when it comes to this man, aren't you?" She smooths her hands over her blanket with a thoughtful expression on her face.

I take a mental picture of her in this moment to look back on whenever I question why I'm doing what I'm doing. "Edgy? Maybe a little. That man has a way of exposing my edges."

She chuckles softly. "I'm sorry. I'm not laughing at you, believe me. It's just the way you're talking about him. I could swear you have a crush."

"Me?" I point to myself. "A crush? I don't think so."

"Which is exactly what people say when they have a crush they don't want anybody to know about." She chuckles. "Don't worry, honey. I won't tell anybody." She pulls an invisible zipper across her lips, then twists an invisible key and tosses it away.

"You might think I have a crush, but I don't," I say firmly. "He is definitely not the sort of person a girl should develop a crush on. There's more to life than a handsome face or a nice body."

"Oh, he has a nice body, too?" Her eyebrows shoot up.

"Mom."

"There's nothing wrong with a…nice body. I was very partial to a nice body when I was your age."

"Mom, you're too much."

"Handsome, nice body. Is he rich? I mean, that would make him every girl's dream."

"Nothing about whether he's a nice person? I thought that was important too."

"Sure, it's important." She winks. "I was going to ask about that next."

I roll my eyes. "Oh, Mom."

"What? It's a valid question. This old lady wants to know if her daughter is going to be taken care of when she's gone."

I frown. "You're not old, Mom and you're not going anywhere for a many years to come. Remember, you said you wanted to see your grandchildren."

She shakes her head. "I asked a simple question."

"Well, to be honest, I really don't know if he has money or not. He drives a nice car and he has a big motorcycle."

"Ooh, a motorcycle. You didn't mention a motorcycle. I need to meet this hunk." She runs a hand over the side of her face, then grins. "Though I don't exactly look my best right now."

"You're always beautiful," I tell her, leaning over to pat her other hand. "So like I said, maybe he has a little money, or he did, but he seems to be just as desperate for cash as I am."

CHAPTER 11

DAKOTA

"How do you know?" she asks, looking at me curiously.

"Uh … we're both doing the same work. We're—umm—sort of working together."

"Oh, I see. Now the pieces of the puzzle are falling into place. Thrown together by destiny, both of you working toward the same goal. Falling in love while you do everything you can to make money and improve your life."

"You're a hopeless romantic. Sometimes I think all those cheesy romance movies you love have warped your brain. Life doesn't really work that way."

"You can't believe that." She grows suddenly serious. Very serious. "You used to believe in true love. It's the only thing that makes life worth living. When you've had a terrible day and the wolf is at the door, wanting money for the gas, electric, phone, the mortgage, and you just don't know where it's going to come from, it is love that keeps you going. When your boss is a bastard and makes you wonder why you even bother working for him in the first place, all you have to do is go home and look into your daughter's innocent eyes." She sighs deeply. "Suddenly, even all the bastards in the world cannot take away the true joy of life because of her sweet smile. Hell, when you miss the bus and it starts pissing down with rain and of course, you left your umbrella at work, you walk home from the bus station to your house soaked and frozen, then you open your door, and there's your baby safe and sound, and it warms you up from the inside out. Love is everything, Dakota. Everything."

"Oh, Mom."

"I'm serious. I'll be gone soon and you need to find someone for yourself. A man. Someone to turn to when times are tight. Somebody to lean on and share your troubles with."

"I'm not interested in getting a man, Mom. I can take care of myself and right now my priority is you."

"Every woman needs someone. You don't know how many times I've wished I had one. Somebody to help ease the burden a little. I don't mean just financially, but...you know...emotionally."

I can't help but feel a little guilty and sad for her when she talks about her wasted life. "I held you back from finding that kind of happiness didn't I?"

"Absolutely not."

"What do you call it, then? No man wanted a woman with a kid, no matter how young you were or how pretty you were. If anything, they were too young to want to be tied down."

"It just isn't true. I didn't have the time for it." She shrugs. "Maybe I was too busy. Maybe I fooled myself into thinking there wasn't the time. You were my world. You still are. I couldn't give myself to anybody else when I gave so much to you."

"So that still makes it my fault."

"You're a stubborn girl."

"You're a stubborn woman," I shoot back.

She tuts and shakes her head. "Of all the things to pass onto you. My stubborn streak had to be it."

"You passed on a lot more than that."

We fall into an easy silence as we both turn our attention to the TV. A game show, of course. Unlike the game show I'm on, where the organizers tried to make us steal. Thank God, she never watches the new stuff. Only reruns of the shows from the time she was a girl. I guess it's a nostalgic thing with her. I know I can't keep Dare Me a secret from her forever. Besides, I'll eventually have to tell her about the money. She'll want to know where it came from. A few thousand dollars could be explained away without much effort. A million? A whole different story.

"So, about this young man…" she says in a sing-song tone as soon as we reach a commercial break.

"I should've known you wouldn't let it go that easily," I groan, never looking away from the TV.

"When are you going to bring him around for supper?"

My head whirls around in her direction. "I'm not. Not ever. Absolutely not."

Her face falls. "Because you don't want him to see me like this?"

"Of course not!" I reply, stunned. "I'm not ashamed of you. I'd take you to meet the Queen of England if I could. What I meant was that there's no point in inviting him to dinner when he would never come." I feel a bit sad as I say this. "There wouldn't be a reason for him to. It would be extremely irregular for me to do something like that."

"You don't get along with him?"

"He's totally impossible. I already told you that."

Her smile is wise, knowing, gentle. "Ah, a bit of a prick, is he?"

"Mom," I gasp.

"Even bad boys can be warmed up. Never say never."

I shake my head. How do I explain it to her in a way that she'll understand? I can't keep dancing around the truth of the subject with her. "The thing is, Mom. He's sort of my competition. Even though we're on the same team for now, that won't always be the case. Eventually, if we keep doing as well as we're doing, we'll have to compete against each other."

"Oh. I see. You can't get too close to the competition."

"Exactly. It wouldn't work."

"Because you'll eventually have to turn on each other, and you don't want your feelings for him to get in the way."

"Yes." I smile bravely. While I was riding on the back of his bike, I forgot that small fact. "See. I knew you'd understand."

As long as she doesn't ask too many questions about specifics. I can't imagine what she must think I'm doing.

"Sure. I understand." Her smile widens innocent and full of joy. "But you know something? It works both ways."

"What does?"

"Becoming so close to somebody that you don't want to do what you know needs to be done to beat them. You're not the only person on your little team of two who could fall victim to that phenomena."

My eyes open wide. "Mom. Do you know what you're implying?"

"Oh, sweetness. I'm not implying. I'm saying it straight out. You wanna win? You might have to allow him to catch feelings for you. Who knows? It could work in your favor." She drops a broad wink. "Besides, if he's half as handsome as you say he is, it might not be all bad. You might even enjoy it."

"I cannot, and I mean *cannot*, believe we're having this conversation!" I bend forward, burying my head in my hands.

"Oh, come on, Dakota. I taught you about the birds and the bees."

"Yes, I know," I say with a wry smile. "I remember it vividly to this day."

"Come, come. We're both adults."

"Sorry, but that doesn't make it any less uncomfortable."

"I'm not asking you prostitute yourself for the sake of

winning. Just, you know, let him see you for the beautiful girl you are. Be a little extra…well…friendly. Win him over."

"I have never been more embarrassed in my life, and that's saying something." Especially, considering what I just did this morning. "I feel like this conversation needs to come to an end before you say anything that will scar me for life."

She laughs. "All right. All right. Kids nowadays are too PC." She shrugs before turning up the volume on the TV. "I'll keep all my wisdom to myself then, and you won't be able to benefit from it."

"That works for me. I'll fix you some lunch," I say, standing up.

Anything to get out of that room. I know she's only half-serious. She's my mom, and it's her job to tease me, make me uncomfortable, then laugh at the way I blush and stammer. Actually, I'm glad we had something to talk about other than how sick she feels and how worried she is about paying for treatment. I'm glad she's in such a good mood.

Mom thinks I should let him develop feelings for me, so he won't be able to compete against me when the time comes. That's all well and good—but she doesn't know him, and she doesn't know the way we are together. He'll never like me. We're always at each other's throats, always getting under each other's skin.

Skin.

My heart picks up speed when I remember his skin, the way it felt under my hands when I slid them around his waist and clasped them over his steely abs. I fought off the burning urge to run my lips over his broad back. I just blamed it on biology. On the deep, pulsing throb between my legs. That was the engine's fault. It would have happened no matter who was driving that motorcycle. There's nothing I could have done about that. If I had taken the bus home like I'd expected to, there wouldn't have been a problem. I wouldn't have lost my head and wouldn't be thinking these thoughts.

No. He'll never come so close to making a fool of himself over me as I did over him. He's too arrogant, too good-looking, too confident, and way too focused. It's that focus I have to worry about, not his smile, his sexy eyes, or the way his butt looked in my underwear.

He won't stop at anything to win this game. I saw it in his eyes when the text arrived that we would have to steal. He was willing to do it. If he hadn't come up with an alternative, he would have stolen the clothes without hesitation.

I wonder why he needs the money so bad. There has to be a reason, though I can't imagine what it would be. I suppose we all have our reasons, don't we?

Still, it was fun to work with him this morning. He's a good teammate. And even when we were making fun of each other and slinging barbs back and forth, I had a good time. He's exciting, interesting, and smart as hell. I can't remember the last time I enjoyed the company of a guy. Maybe never. Even when he is being an insufferable jackass, and he does that a lot, I want to be with him. The thing is...I can be myself around him. I haven't tried to flirt with him or make him like me, and I won't. I'll win this game fair and square.

I smile to myself as I spread tuna salad on a slice of wheat bread for Mom's lunch. He should have looked ridiculous in my boy shorts, but he looked devastatingly hot. I never thought I'd ever meet a man like him, one who can look good even when he is making a ridiculous fool of himself.

I'm frowning again, as I slap another slice of bread on top and cut the sandwich in half. He is *so* out of my league. Still, he did say I looked hot too, didn't he? I almost wish I didn't like that so much. That it didn't make me feel so warm and gooey inside.

I hear Mom start coughing out in the living room—the sort of cough that starts out as a laugh but goes out of control. And that's enough to snap me out of my little daydreams, the memories of the fun with Trent. He's not important. His body isn't important, his motorcycle isn't important. The way he feels about me isn't important, either. Whether he really thinks I'm hot, or if he thinks I'm a heinous bitch. None of it matters more than my mother. She's my priority. She's the reason I have to win. I don't care what his reasons are.

My fingers tighten around the bread knife until it hurts. "You alright in there?" I call out when the coughing eases, trying to keep my voice as light as possible so she doesn't tell me not to worry so much.

"Sure, I'm alright. You know how it is." She sounds weaker than she did earlier. Worn out.

Yes. I know exactly how it is.

CHAPTER 12

"**C**aveman & Bone?" Dakota asks looking up from her text message, a scowl on her face. "That's a strip joint, isn't it?" We are both standing on the street two doors away from the club when they sent us our messages.

I scratch my jaw. "Yeah, I think so," I say cautiously.

"They want me to do a strip tease, don't they?" she gasps, horrified.

"Well, we don't know that," I suggest diplomatically, even though it's pretty certain that she is right. That's exactly what they want her to do.

"It's obvious... it is. Why else would they want us to go there?" she wails.

I try to keep my face neutral even though, to be perfectly honest, I wouldn't mind seeing her strip. From the moment I saw her run for the elevator, I became sexually curious about her. "Let's go in and see."

"Trent, I'm not getting naked in front of a bunch of men. I'm just not doing it." Her voice is high and squeaky.

"Okay look, my friend Eric goes to Caveman & Bone all the time. It's more of a topless show. You can keep your panties on."

"What? I have to be topless?" she shoots back.

I swallow down a sigh. "A few moments ago, you thought you would have to be naked. Isn't being topless better than stripping all the way down?"

"Oh my God, I don't believe this! I'll have to be topless in public?"

"I stripped down to my underpants yesterday," I remind her.

"You don't have breasts, you unfeeling brute," she rages.

"Well, at least you have great breasts."

Her eyes look like they are about to pop out of her head. "Fuck you and the horse you rode in on, Trent."

Holy Hell! "That's too hard? Here's another alternative, Tinkerbell. Why not just go back to Neverland and let someone else win the million?"

That stops her in her tracks. She licks her lips and squares her shoulders. "All right, let's go in and see what they want us to do."

"Good thinking."

We don't exchange another word while we walk into the establishment. Her body is stiff and there is at least two feet between us.

As if they are expecting us, the two bouncers at the entrance lift the red ropes as soon as we appear, and let us through.

There are two women sitting at the reception area who also seem to be expecting us. One of them gets up and asks if she can take our coats.

I hand mine over, but Dakota holds hers even tighter.

We follow the woman into the club.

The plum carpets are plush and the décor is rich and lavish. There's a stage lit up with blue lights and a long catwalk attached to it. I sneak a glance at Dakota. Her hands are thrust deep into her short coat and she is staring at the stage with terrified eyes. At the other end of the room, there is a long bar and lots of scantily clad girls are sitting around waiting for the unwary.

The woman leads us to a table by the stage.

As soon as we sit, a waitress dressed in a playboy bunny suit minus the tail and ears brings us a bucket of ice with a champagne bottle in it. "With compliments of the house," she says setting our glasses down on the table.

Dakota stares at the bottle as if it is a rattlesnake.

The stage lights come on and the DJ asks everyone to welcome, the next performer. A Miss Susie Wong. Men in the darkened corners of the club clap. An Oriental girl in a long green Chinese dress comes on and starts gyrating to the music.

Dakota stares at the performer with mesmerized eyes.

With a practiced ease, the girl slips out of her dress. She has fake boobs, but a nice body. Tight, young, and well proportioned, but for some reason, she leaves me completely cold. I don't like the idea of paying to watch a girl undress. I have better ways to spend my money.

With admirable athletic prowess, she vaults herself up a lapdancer's pole and swings herself around it before losing her bra. At that point, men start throwing money at her. She gets down on her hands and knees then starts crawling to the end of the catwalk. Men come up to the edge of it to slip folded notes into her stockings and G-string. Finally, she gets to the end of the catwalk where she lies on her back and opens her legs, making a large V.

Next to me, Dakota gasps.

I watch the men shower the girl with notes. This is obviously the highlight of the show.

Dakota turns to me, her face white and desperate. "I can't do it. That's humiliating."

"You don't know what they want you to do. It might be something completely different. Why don't you have a drink and loosen up a little, huh?"

She grabs her glass and drains it.

I refill her glass silently. If she has to dance, then getting her a little drunk is a good idea.

She finishes the glass just as soon as I refill it. I pour her another, and she empties that too.

My eyes widen. Getting her falling down drunk is not going to help anybody. "Easy now," I caution.

"Easy for you to say," she snaps bitterly.

At that moment, my phone buzzes. We look at each other in surprise. Only my phone! I look at my screen.

Good Evening Dare Me Contestant!
Time for your next Dare Me stunt.
Eat everything that is in the bowl.
The value of this dare is $100,000

CHAPTER 13

TRENT

W hat? I look up confused and another tailless, earless bunny is carrying a tray with a bowl on it. She puts it in front of me.

Oh. Fuck. No.

Even Dakota jerks back in disgust.

I stare at the contents of the bowl in disbelief. I know exactly what's in the bowl. It hits me then. The organizers of Dare Me have trawled my social media account. Years ago, a friend sent me a video of a South Vietnam delicacy. *'How to prepare and eat live coconut worms.'*

I can't take my eyes off the fat worms squirming in a concoction of chilies, lime juice, and some other Asian sauces. I remember clearly leaving a comment on the video. 'I'd rather die than eat that.' Now they are going to use it against me. My stomach begins to churn.

"Jesus, do they want you to eat *that*?" Dakota asks.

I nod slowly.

"You should eat them quick. This is cruel. Those poor things must be burning up in that chili soup."

Un-fucking-believable. Of course, she would care more for the wellbeing of the damn worms than mine. I look up at her and snarl, "Fine, I'll eat them, but make sure you do your stunt just as quickly when it's your turn."

She shrinks back.

I stare at her. "Do we have a deal?"

She bites her bottom lip.

"Do we have a deal?" I repeat.

"Yes," she whispers.

I pick up the chopsticks lying at the side of the bowl and take a deep breath. Nothing is more important than winning this game. Nothing is more important than my dream. *Nothing.* I catch one of the wriggling worm between my chopsticks.

Without looking at it again, I bring it into my mouth and crunch it quickly between my teeth. I don't allow myself to feel sick. Without acknowledging the milky taste bursting onto my tongue, I swallow the still wriggling mass. I feel it go down my throat and travel into my esophagus. There is a lingering taste of chili and fish sauce in my mouth. My toes curl in my shoes.

I just ate a worm that was still alive.

I look into the bowl. There are five more. I do the same until my bowl is empty of them. I look at up Dakota.

She is staring at me with wide eyes. "I'd rather take my clothes off than do that," she whispers. Her phone buzzes.

She looks at it, then up to me. Her face is pale. She looks nothing like that girl I met in the carpark.

"What is your stunt?"

"I have to dance until I have collected two hundred dollars from the men here. Wish me luck." She takes off her coat. She is wearing a denim dress with thick tights.

Inexplicably and suddenly, I don't want her to be up there. Dancing and having all these perverts staring at her. I don't want to see her breasts. I mean, I do of course, but not like this. She is too good for this.

A woman comes up to her. "I can escort you to the back where you can change into your costume."

Dakota nods. Her shoulders are no longer straight. They are slumped and defeated. She stands up and follows the woman.

I don't even have to think. I open my wallet. There's less than a hundred in cash. I can run out and look for cash, but I might disqualify myself. I put my wallet back into my pocket, and think fast. I pull out my phone and call Eric. He lives around the corner from here.

"Where are you?" I ask.

"Just about to go out to dinner, man. Where are you?"

"Can you get to the Caveman?"

"Sure. Are you at the Caveman?" he asks incredulously.

"Yeah, can you bring two hundred dollars with you?"

"What's going on?" he asks confused.

"I'll tell you everything later. Just get here as soon as you can."

"Okay."

"How long will you be?" I ask in a panicked voice.

"I don't know. Twenty minutes."

"Okay. Hurry up." I slip my phone back into my pocket and look at my watch. *Come on, Eric. Get here fast.* I tap my fingers on the table surface impatiently.

Ten minutes later, things start happening on the stage. The DJ takes his place. The curtain twitches. Shit, she's coming on. The bright stage lights come on and the DJ announces her name.

Fuck.

I call Eric again. "Where the fuck are you?"

"I'm just around the corner, dude. I'm getting the money out of the hole in the wall."

"Hurry up, please."

"I'll be there in five."

"Make it four," I growl.

The music starts and Dakota appears in the spotlight. She is wearing a red top that seems to be made of mesh with a tie between her breasts, a pair of white go-go shorts, and knee length black boots. The men start catcalling and whistling. Her face looks pale and nervous under all the makeup they have slapped on her. Her enormous eyes desperately look for me in the dark.

I stand and smile encouragingly.

When she knows I'm there her eyes slide away.

It is a shock to me how protective I feel of her. I sit down, my hand gripping the seat so hard, it hurts. If one guy says one bad thing…I look around me.

Men are starting to move towards the catwalk. They're attracted by the idea of a new dancer, fresh meat.

Dakota starts to move to the music, her movements are jerky. She goes to the pole and swings around it the way the Asian girl had done, but in a shaky, amateurish way.

Someone whistles, someone else laughs.

I feel my hands clench with fury. I force myself to breathe slowly. Eric will be here soon. He will come with the money and I will stop this travesty. I stare at her. Under the spotlight, she glows like something unreal. An angel. She tugs at the tie under her breasts and it comes loose. She shrugs out of it as she walks down the catwalk. Underneath, she is wearing a tiny red bikini top.

Her eyes meet mine.

I can't breathe.

She turns around and fuck—she has an amazing ass. Problem is, I'm not the only one seeing it.

Someone calls out, "Whoa, sugar, that's one fine ass you have!"

I see red. Jealousy burns my gut. I stand and walk over to him.

He is sitting with a group of men. They are obviously city boys out for a night of fun.

I want to knock his head off, but I know that will just get me kicked out. "Can you fucking keep your comments to yourself?" I snarl furiously.

"Fuck you," he retorts.

I'm about to lose it when I hear Eric's voice call out to me. I turn around and stride over to him. "Have you got the money?"

"Yeah." He stares at me, surprised, as if he's seeing me for the first time.

"Go give it to the girl on the stage."

"Yeah?"

"Yeah. Hurry up," I almost yell.

Eric runs over to the catwalk and holds the money out to Dakota.

She understands immediately. She reaches out, grabs the money, and holds it up. 'I've got it. I've got the two hundred dollars!"

My phone buzzes. I look at it and hold the phone triumphantly aloft so Dakota can see the lighted up message.

"Congratulation! You have both completed your Dare Me stunts successfully.
You both up by $210,000!

CHAPTER 14

TRENT

I have to admit, I'm still riding high.

Completing that first stunt gave me the forward momentum I needed. Conquering my revulsion finishing that bowl of live worms, then getting Eric to come with the money has given me new confidence. I know now I can handle whatever they throw at me. As I wait for Dakota outside the Italian restaurant we were instructed to meet at, I can't help but wonder if she experienced the same rush I did after the first stunt.

I remember the pressure of her arms around my waist, the feel of her body behind me, and the way she squeezed me when we got word, we'd passed the first challenge. Yes. She felt it, too.

The image of her wearing nothing but my shirt skims around the fringe of my consciousness. A woman wearing your shirt is like a flag on a body you've conquered. I haven't conquered her... but I want to. Badly. No matter how many times I've tried to shut down that train of thought, she manages to pop up someplace else. Her smooth long legs. I wanted to tell her to take it off when we reached the garage where my motorcycle was parked, knowing I was still holding her bra with the rest of her clothes.

Sure, she would've slapped me, but it would have been worth it.

She might not be as bad as I thought she was either. She's still prickly and sarcastic, but I'm sarcastic too, so it works. What really got to me was she's willing to make a fool of herself, which I kinda admire. In my experience, even the girls who consider themselves free spirits will balk at the idea of going against socially acceptable behavior. Not her. She was fun. I had a good time with her. I stop myself short. Thinking about her this way is getting me nowhere. I shouldn't be doing it.

I glance into the restaurant through the window. It doesn't look crowded, but then it's an out-of-the-way place without much foot traffic. I wonder why they sent us here.

"Hey Rich Boy," she says, appearing behind me out of nowhere.

I jump. "You'll give someone a heart attack, if you're not careful." What is it about this woman that brings out the worst in me. I'm not really an ass, but she turns me into one. Or maybe I'm an ass and I just didn't know it?

She rolls her eyes. "Yeah okay, Grandpa." She looks up at the sign with a frown. "What's the deal with this place anyway? I've never heard of it."

"Neither have I." I shrug.

"Are we supposed to like, strip down, walk in and ask for service?" she smirks.

The idea has a certain appeal to it, and I raise an eyebrow. "Maybe you should give that a shot, see what happens."

"No, thanks."

Just then, our phones go off.

She pulls hers out with a sigh.

> **Welcome to your third Dare Me stunt.**
> **Go inside and order over a thousand**
> **dollars' worth of food and drink.**
> *Finish every single thing you order."*
> *You must finish your stunt in two*
> *hours or sooner. Good luck.*

"Good thing I'm hungry," I mutter as I slide my phone into my pocket.

"Do you know how much a thousand dollars' worth of food is? And Italian food is so heavy. That much food could probably last me a whole month," she whispers worriedly.

I look down at her anxious face. "Relax, we'll order the most expensive stuff. That way, we can eat less."

"I hope we can eat everything."

"We'll have to. I don't care if my stomach bursts, I'm finishing every last drop."

"They don't expect us to pay for this, do they?" she asks with a frown.

"Didn't you read the contract? They'll reimburse us for expenses."

"Right. I didn't get a chance to yet. I hope you have the money, because my credit card is maxed out."

"Yeah, I got it." I go to the door and open it for her, and she steps inside. It's a cozy little place. Cozy's a good word for it too. The décor is homely and a bit faded. It has the feel of a family run business.

"All it needs is the guy on an accordion," she whispers with a half-smile.

"Huh?"

"Lady and the Tramp." She looks up and frowns at the blank expression on my face. "You know…the famous scene of Lady and Tramp sharing the bowl of spaghetti."

I stare at her blankly.

"God. Did you even have a childhood?"

I'm about to fire off a retort when a server comes by to seat us. There are only ten, maybe twelve tables in the place and only two of them are currently in use. I have to wonder why we couldn't just seat ourselves. I smile as we're led to our table and a list of specials is rattled off. I stop just short of asking which specials are the most expensive.

I scan the wine list first. That's where I'm hoping we'll blow a great potion of the most money. They don't have a bad wine list. Nothing too jaw-dropping, but respectable for such a small place.

"Wow, it's a big menu," Dakota murmurs to herself as she scans the dinner menu.

"Filet, lobster, seabass…" I read aloud. "Okay. We can handle this."

"Can we?" She peers at me over the top of the menu with a frown.

"Oh, come on. Have a little fun. When's the last time somebody told you to order the most expensive items on the menu?" I remember the neighborhood I dropped her off in. I remember the house. She's not exactly dirt poor, but she's definitely not rolling in it, and her credit cards are all maxed out.

"Fun? My stomach is churning with anxiety." She looks around warily. "Are there cameras on us now?"

"I think we'd better get used to having cameras on us at all times. It's easier to assume they're always there,"

"Doesn't it freak you out a little, though? The thought that there's somebody watching us all the time. Not just one somebody, either, but a whole lot of them."

I shrug. "Quite frankly. I don't care. The whole damn world can watch if they want. I just want to win the money."

"I suppose you're used to people staring at you all the time."

"Don't tell me you're not used to people looking at you all the time."

"What's that supposed to mean?" she asks, eyes narrowed in suspicion.

"Jesus, are you always so quick take offence? All I meant was, you're not exactly ugly. I'm sure you attract your fair share of attention."

"Not exactly ugly? Stop, or I'll have to climb across the table and bury my fork in your skull," she warns, but I catch the slight glimpse of a smile before she hides it by raising the menu in front of her face.

CHAPTER 15

TRENT

The waiter who seated us greets us, "Good evening, Sir. Is there anything I can start you off with tonight?"

Dakota's at a total loss. Time for me to step up. "Sure is. We're celebrating tonight, so we'll have a bottle of your finest Champagne, followed by your Barolo Riserva."

The man's eyes light up. "Certainly, certainly."

"For our entrée, I think we'll share a charcuterie plate and an order of oysters, but only if they're extremely fresh."

"We just had a new shipment arrive today," he announces with a broad smile.

"Yes, I'm sure you had. I'll have six of those, but I can't stop looking at your seared diver scallops, either. So I'll have a portion of that too." I look down at the menu. "Do you have black truffles?"

"Yes, Sir. We certainly do."

"How much would you charge me for a plate of pasta covered in black truffles?"

His eyebrows fly up to his receding hairline. "Covered, Sir?"

"Absolutely covered." I grin. "I don't mind paying, so don't be shy about charging me the full price."

"Well, sir. For a normal portion we'd charge thirty dollars, but if you want it covered then perhaps… sixty dollars?"

"I'd like you to double the amount of truffles in my dish and charge me one hundred and twenty dollars for it."

He gulps, his Adam's apple moving visibly. "Sure. I can do that."

"Honey, you said you wanted lobster tonight, didn't you?"

"Mm-hmm," she nods, smiling up at the waiter. She's finally playing along. "Yes, I would love the lobster fra diavolo, please. And a side order of garlic spinach. Oh, and garlic bread, too."

"Oof," I groan with a wink. "Not too much of the garlic bread, honey, First of all, it will fill you up too quickly and secondly, I won't be able to kiss you later tonight."

The waiter's eyes nearly fall out of his head.

Dakota blushes charmingly, then spoils it by kicking me really hard under the table. While I try not to rub my shin, she smiles innocently at the waiter. "Yes, my husband is right, please cancel that garlic bread, but add extra garlic to the spinach." She shoots me a defiant look and I laugh.

The waiter scribbles furiously on his notepad before turning to me again.

"Hmm… let's see. For my main course, I'd like the twelve-ounce filet mignon with asparagus. I'll take the lobster tail add-on with that too, but I'm a sucker for risotto too." I glance at Dakota.

"Why not get both?" she suggests.

"Good thinking, darling." I snap the menu shut with a satisfied smile. "Yes. I'll take both."

"Both?"

We've ordered around six hundred dollars of food and alcohol so far, if my math is correct. "Yes. Both. Oh, and salads, too. Of course." I hand him the menus with a smile and hope my appetite is ready for what I'm about to throw at it. Good thing I've got antacids in the medicine cabinet back home.

The thing is, the food is excellent. Beyond excellent.

"Wow, this pasta is homemade," Dakota says with a happy smile. "And the sauce? Oh, my God." She goes in for a second bite, then takes a sip of her wine. "It's all so fresh," she waxes. "So delicious. And all free. We don't have to pay for a thing."

I hide a smile. I like Dakota after two glasses of champagne and one and a half glasses of wine. She is all mellow and dreamy. "I know. I'm pretty sure my oysters were just put on ice this afternoon."

"I don't know how you can eat those," she grimaces, shaking her head.

"And I don't know how you could consume so much garlic and spinach in one meal but hey, I'm not judging."

She doesn't even bother defending herself, because she's too busy making out with a lobster claw. "Oh, man, this is delicious. I've never had lobster before."

"Never?"

"Nope." She licks her fingers.

"Let's hope you're not allergic."

She smiles dreamily. "It would be worth it."

I can't help smiling. It's nice, seeing her enjoy herself. I didn't know until now, how tired I was of watching women pretending not to enjoy their food.

She dives in with gusto and doesn't stop until she's mopping up the plate with a piece of bread.

"Save room for dessert. You know we'll have to order some more," I remind her, as I signal for more wine. That, plus dessert, should bring the bill to just over a thousand. I'm feeling a little buzzed. More than a little. I drank most of the champagne and the red wine. But it's not a bad feeling. I could get used to this. I'll have to get a taxi to take me home rather than driving.

"I don't know if I can squeeze in another bite," she groans, both hands over her stomach. "You're gonna have to roll me out of here. I can't believe I made such a pig of myself."

"And on camera, too," I tease.

"Ouch."

"Whatever. Enjoy yourself." I want to add. *Enjoy yourself for once.* I'm starting to get the impression that there isn't much joy in her life. Not that I would know joy if it jumped up and bit me on the ass, but I at least know how to let loose and have fun without obsessing over the price of the smallest luxuries.

CHAPTER 16

TRENT

For the last course, we both order tiramisu and cappuccino. "And I'd love a nice port, if you have one," I add at the last minute.

"Me, too," Dakota agrees.

I'm pretty sure our waiter thinks he's died and gone to heaven—meanwhile, if my math is correct, with the additional wine I ordered with our entrees we're up over a thousand dollars. I hope that's enough for whatever the audience wants from us. The table could only hold so much food at one time.

Instead of the waiter bringing our port, a woman with white-streaked hair and a sweet smile brings the two glasses on a small tray. "I just had to come out and meet the two of you for myself, to prove you're real," she chuckles.

"What do you mean?" Dakota asks, glancing at me.

"I don't think we've ever had a check like yours with only two people dining," she laughs. She just can't keep the smile off her face. "We're going to have a good night, thanks to the two of you."

"I'm glad. The food was fantastic." There is something motherly and kind about her and it makes me smile.

"Yes, it's getting harder for us now. We're not bright or shiny and you'll be surprised how easy it is for people to walk right past this place," she continues, a frown touching her face. "If it weren't for my granddaughter's tuition, I would sell and retire. I'm old and tired and it is just not worth it anymore, but my daughter died a few years ago and Jessica needs the money for school so I carry on, but I can tell you some days are so bad, I'm not sure we'll make it. Then you two come in and turn things around and now I have hope for tomorrow. Your bill will pay the wages for this week."

"You're so sweet to come out and speak with us," Dakota says, hands crossed over her chest.

"And you're very sweet for making an old lady so happy. Thank you both." She signals to one of the waiters for our desserts to arrive. "Your desserts and coffee are on the house."

Both Dakota and I speak up at the same time.

"Absolutely not," I say.

"We wouldn't dream of not paying for our dessert and coffee," Dakota chimes in.

"Oh," she exclaims, surprised by how instant and unanimous our objection is. "But I would like to give you something complimentary."

Dakota shakes her head. "No, no, it's not necessary. We

prefer to pay for them. Please do us a favor and charge us for everything."

"Are you sure?" she asks doubtfully.

"It will make us happy," Dakota says softly.

Suddenly, she turns towards me and holds out her hand, her eyes full of gratitude. "You are such amazing young people. If only there were more people like you in the world. Thank you."

"No, thank you for a great meal," I say. I'm too full to move, but what a great night it has been. Dakota was funny and easy-going, the food was to die for, and we managed to help a sweet lady too.

"Wow," Dakota whispers when we're alone again. Her face is glowing. "I feel like puking, but this has been a really great night, and I'm so glad we made her happy."

I groan when a plate of tiramisu appears in front of me. Dakota laughs at my expression. It's okay for her since I've eaten the lion's share of all the food we ordered, but I'm so damn full, I can hardly move. I pick up the spoon with steely determination. This is the last thing, I tell myself as I start at it.

A burb erupts from deep within me and Dakota's eyes widen, but I keep spooning the creamy concoction. I'll burst before I give up.

After a few minutes, I say, "That's it. We're done." I put the spoon down. I've never felt so uncomfortably full in my whole life, but we've completed our stunt.

"We just won't eat for a week," Dakota says with a grin as our phones both signal a new text.

I look at my phone

My overly full stomach sinks when I read the message.

Time to dine and dash!
Get out of there NOW
without getting caught!
Your prize: $100,000!

We stare at each other in horror.

Dakota actually becomes pale. "What the hell, Trent?" she whispers. "This can't be real. What kind of monsters are running this game show?"

"Fuck," I swear, pissed at myself for not seeing it sooner. Why else would they make us order all this food and rack up such a huge bill? They could have sent us to McDonald's if they just wanted us to get sick on food.

"Are we going to do this?" she asks, staring at me with wide eyes. "I mean, that poor woman..."

"...And her granddaughter. I know. It would've been bad enough if she hadn't come out to thank us."

"She shook hands with you, Trent."

"I know. I know." I avoid looking at Dakota's face and try to think. Shit. Shit. Shit. I can't believe I fell for it. There's no way around it. I now look at Dakota's pale face. "We don't have a choice. We have to do it unless we want to give up now. Do you?"

She closes her eyes for a second and grimaces. "Ugh. We can't do that."

"I know."

She bites her bottom lip and looks around to where the woman is sitting at a table writing something in a book. "Oh, God. If we do this to her, she is going to lose her faith in humanity."

"We have to go through with it," I say firmly.

She covers her face with her hands. "I suppose we do, but I feel sick."

When our smiling waiter comes by with our check, my chest feels tight and uncomfortable. This is so wrong.

"How much?" Dakota asks.

"One thousand, one hundred and twenty-five dollars."

She closes her eyes. "And I'm sure he's looking for a tip, too."

"Of course. We'll ruin everybody's night, but it's between staying on the show or leaving it."

"You don't have to tell me." She glances around again.

"There's hardly anybody out here. Why don't you go out, pretend you have a call to take, and I'll follow shortly. Once I'm out of here, run."

"Run where?" she whispers, eyes enormous.

"I don't know. Just run. I'll follow."

"I'm not sure I can run after eating all this…"

"So find an alley to throw up in. But run." I sit back, waiting for her to leave.

Pulling her phone out and holding it to her ear like she's answering a call, she walks to the door of the restaurant. I watch, trying to look as casual as possible, drumming my fingers on the tabletop. When enough time has passed, I get up and follow her out the door with my heart slamming like crazy against my ribcage.

"Go! Go! Go!" We take off at a run, across the street.

Within seconds, the sound of two angry voices follows us and I dare shoot a look over my shoulder. A man in a Chef's uniform and our waiter. They are screaming and waving their arms, cursing up a storm.

"Run!" I gasp, overtaking her, grabbing her hand, and pulling her faster. Either the food is weighing her down or she's just damn slow, but the two from the restaurant aren't slow and they want their money. I don't blame them.

We cut down an alley and I yank her behind a dumpster at the last second, pressing her to the wall with a finger to her lips. Our pursuers either didn't see us, or gave up. Neither of them looked like they were in great shape. I count to one hundred in my head, slowly, before I feel even remotely safe.

"We lost them," she pants, pressing against me.

I'm leaning against her too, trying to hide the two of us in the stinking alley, next to a smelly dumpster. But it's not that I'm thinking of right now. I'm not even thinking about the restaurant or the sweet old lady whose wonderful night we just ruined.

I'm thinking about her. How gorgeous she is. Those thickly

lashed hazel eyes are staring up into mine with a vulnerable, totally fuckable expression. I hear the sound of her heart beating, and smell her perfume. Or it could be her lip balm. Something fruity. I feel her firm breasts pressing into my abs. We're standing so close I feel myself swallowing her quick, jerky hot breaths. They smell of coffee, mascarpone cheese, and champagne.

Suddenly, I'm breathing as hard as she is. And it's not the running that's done it.

Our phones buzz, reminding me of why we're there. It's not for a fucking make out session.

Dakota blinks suddenly, and the moment's over. She stays still as a statue while I reach for my device.

"Congratulations," I read out. "You've successfully completed your second Dare Me stunt, and moved up in the ranks. You are each $100,000 richer. Good luck on your next stunt."

I look at her.

She looks at me.

We're through to the next level. So why are neither of us happy about it?

CHAPTER 17

DAKOTA

I feel sick. Depressed. Ashamed of myself. A hundred thousand dollars. I can hardly wrap my head around the number, even when I know there's so much more to come. But it means nothing, really. Just a stepping stone. It could become smoke if we don't get to the next level and all of this would have been for nothing. "Congratulations, I guess," I mumble.

"Yeah. Same to you." He shrugs. "Well, we had to do it. We didn't exactly have a choice, if we want to win."

"I know." I close my eyes against the tears that are threatening to flow. What's wrong with me? I had to do it. I think about Mom and remind myself of how little a choice I have. This is all for her. Sure, we hurt that lady's feelings, but it's not like she won't have plenty of chances to make more money. Our check isn't going to make or break the restaurant. Her granddaughter will still be able to stay in school.

"I know you feel like hell about it," he murmurs, brushing

dark hair out of his eyes where it flopped over while we were running. "And I don't like it, either."

"You don't seem too bothered by it." I glare at him. How can he be so heartless? Stupid me. For a minute there, I fell for his superficial charm and his good looks while I imagined he had a heart. I should've known better. First impressions are usually right, aren't they? And I was right about him. He only pretends to be a nice person. He can turn it on and turn it off as it suits him, depending on the situation and who he's trying to impress.

"What am I supposed to do?" His eyes narrow and his tone turns nasty. "We passed the stunt, we're moving on. This is what we're supposed to do, you know. This is the entire point. Winning."

"Yes, I know," I sneer.

"Now's not the time to grow a sense of honor."

I wish I could claw his eyes out. I want to. I want nothing more than to leave long gashes down the sides of his face and rip those pretty eyes from his head, the snide bastard. "Excuse me, but I already had a sense of honor when I started this process. You don't know why I'm after this money any more than I know why you're after it, but I have a damn good reason. So don't act like I wasn't a good person before this started."

"Tell yourself that all you want," he jeers. "I didn't see you kicking and screaming and dragging your feet, you know. You walked out of that restaurant with that phone to your ear without me shoving you out the door, remember? Don't act so superior when you did exactly the same thing I did."

That stings. It was too easy to leave, wasn't it? "You're the one who had to order all that expensive food." I know how pathetic it sounds even as it's coming out of my mouth, but it's too late to stop myself. I won't back down even though my argument is growing weaker all the time.

His laugh is cold, cruel, and without humor. "And didn't you help eat everything?"

"What was I supposed to do?"

"You never tried to stop me from ordering, either. You were glad that one of us had the balls to go in there and do what we were supposed to do. We just advanced to the next round of the game. You should be thanking me, instead of taking out your sore conscience on me." When he's angry like this, his face changes. He doesn't look so handsome anymore. He's vicious now. Like an animal with its teeth showing.

My blood is boiling to the point where I can barely see straight. But it's not him I'm mad at—at least, not mostly. It's me. He's right. I'm a hypocrite, and I want to push the whole thing off on him. Anything to make me feel better, anything to make me forget that sweet old lady and how happy she was. She liked us. She wanted to tell her granddaughter about us. Well, she'll be telling her, for sure. Just not for the reason she thought she would. "Well, we did it. I guess we should be proud of ourselves."

I slide past him and leave the alley. So what if somebody's still waiting? I almost want them to catch me. I've never felt so ashamed of myself. At any rate, we've already won the money, and there was nothing in the stunt stating that we couldn't get caught after getting away. If anything, I wish I had the opportunity to explain why we did it. Maybe I could get the owner to understand.

"You're just walking away, then?"

"Yes. I'm just walking away from *you*." I glance over my shoulder when I reach the sidewalk.

He's still standing there, still looking like he doesn't understand me.

It's all right. I don't understand myself. "I guess you're not used to women walking away, are you?"

He doesn't reply. Good thing, because I'm too tired to fight. I'm too heartsick, too.

Well, that's the way the world works, or so I try to tell myself as I walk even further away from the restaurant. I need to walk off some of that meal—or binge, rather, which is a much better word to describe it. I'll be walking all night and well into the morning if I hope to burn off even part of it. But walking is still better than going home and facing Mom and knowing that I stole tonight in order to help her get the treatment she needs. She would be so mad at me if she knew. So disappointed. And she'd never forgive herself if she knew I did it for her.

I want to tell myself it was only a meal, just a few hundred bucks. No big deal. Nobody's going to suffer too much over that. I didn't rob the cash register. And I'm sure the food is marked up like crazy, too. If anything, they're robbing the customers by charging what they do.

It's a nice night. Warmer than it's been lately. Funny, how sixty degrees feels warm at the end of winter and chilly at the end of summer. This is the former, and there are happy people walking all over South Philly. The corner BYOBs and trattorias are bustling, full of smiling people and enticing aromas which float out onto the street. Of course, it turns my overly-full stomach at the moment.

Maybe there's a way I can help the restaurant build its popularity. Look at these places, how busy they are. Packed from wall to wall. I bet the food I just overate is tons better than anything they serve. I can help them that way. I can make it up to them.

No. I'm just kidding myself. There's only one thing I can do —if I don't, I won't be able to sleep tonight. And Mom will instantly know I did something wrong. I'm not in the mood for even more lies.

Good thing I have a little cash in my savings account.

Five-twenty-five would be my half for the food and another one-fifty for the waiter. I wince throughout the entire transaction at the ATM. Six-hundred-seventy-five dollars. But hey. I have a theoretical hundred grand waiting for me, right? Somehow, it doesn't help. That's not money I can touch. And if the audience keeps us going along these lines, with even bigger dares and higher consequences, I don't know how much further I'll be able to go. For the first time, I'm genuinely worried that I won't be able to finish the show.

For now, I can make things right. I tuck the money deep into my purse and walk with my head down, moving as fast as I can. Like the faster I walk, the easier it'll be for me to outrun my guilt.

Trent is right. I'll never admit it to him, but he is. I didn't stop him from ordering every expensive thing he could find. I encouraged him. And I ate like a glutton. I enjoyed it. I should've known there was some bigger reason for the stunt, but I wanted to believe in the moment that everything was okay. That we were only having fun, enjoying dinner together.

Truth be told—and my cheeks burn with furious shame when I admit it to myself—I even enjoyed running. Sure, guilt crushed me as soon as I knew we were safe, but the running part was fun. Beating the men, getting away with theft. Trent and I were partners in crime this morning and again tonight. It was exciting. So, what did I do? I took it all out on him. I don't think I've ever felt so mixed-up.

I hope nobody finds out what I'm about to do. Especially him.

I round the corner only a block from the restaurant, and my heart pounds so hard I can barely hear myself think. I have to face them. They hate me. They have to, after what I did. But I have to face them and apologize and I know I can't give the real reason why we ran. I don't want to get disqualified.

I freeze in shock when I see who's coming from further down the street. Trent freezes, too, before sighing. I can tell by the way his shoulders rise and fall. He continues walking toward me, and I wait for him.

"What are you doing?" he asks, looking back and forth like he's afraid we're being watched.

"I was going back to pay the check. Don't get mad at me. It's the right thing to do."

"And what do you think I was doing?" He pulls his wallet from his back pocket and opens it, showing me a stack of hundred-dollar bills. "It took me ages to find an ATM branch for my bank, but I managed."

I don't know whether to laugh, cry or apologize. So I smile, and he does, too.

"I'm sorry I was such a bitch before. I was actually angry with myself and I took it out on you. It wasn't fair."

"You're saying sorry to me?" he asks a delighted expression on his face.

"Don't start," I warn.

The air between us changes. We stand there for what feels like a long time, looking at each other. I remember the breathless, giddy feeling when he stood so close to me in the alley. How I was so sure, he was just seconds away from kissing me. How sure I was that I would let him do it, too. I wanted him to. I craved an excuse to finally find out what his lips tasted like.

"Wanna go Dutch?" I ask.

Trent throws his head back with a laugh. "I'm not usually one to accept when a woman offers to go Dutch, but I think I can make an exception tonight. You're an honest, decent woman, Dakota Manning."

CHAPTER 18

TRENT

She sits on my bed while I watch her from my arm chair. Her cream sweater, yeah, the ridiculous one she wore to the mall, and bra are already off, and she is only in her dark blue jeans. I thought she'd act nervous somehow, but she isn't. She's beautiful beyond my wildest expectations.

Her hair is exactly the way it was that first day I met her. A hot, sexy mess, as if she just got out of bed. Her eyes are painted with pink eyeshadow and lined with brown liner. They look like cat's eyes. The gold flecks in them glow under the light from my bedroom lamps.

She wants to get down on her knees and suck me off, but I tell her I want a slow, deliberate reveal. I want to draw out and capture every delicious moment. So she leans back, sensuous as a cat, and opens the button of her jeans. She brings the zipper down. Slowly.

"Are you wet?" I ask.

"Soaking," she replies, biting her bottom lip. Seductive. Very seductive.

Fuck, I'm so goddamn hard, I hurt.

With a secret little smile, she lifts her bottom and wriggles those skin-tight jeans out from under her ass and down her legs, while I watch her fascinated. She is wearing one of her boy's shorts again. I'm used to women in lacey thongs, but hell, nothing is sexier than Dakota in boy shorts.

"Open your legs," I order.

She obeys, spreading them nice and wide, and I see the wet patch in the crotch of her panties.

"Lightly scratch your clit through the material."

"Like this?" she asks innocently. There's something dirty about a woman scratching her clit through her panties.

"Exactly like that. That's it. Back and forth. Back and forth."

She moans and arches her back, lifting those ripe breasts. Oh, beautiful.

"Keep scratching baby. Keep scratching that clit. And keep your legs spread open."

"Mmmmm…" she moans.

"Now push the material aside and show me your tight little cunt."

She obeys instantly.

I like this Dakota. No back chat. No pig-headed objections. Just a wonderfully responsive submissive sex toy. She hooks a finger into the side of her panties, pulls back, and exposes her pink pussy to me.

I fist my swollen cock and lazily pump myself.

She watches me masturbating. Her eyes wide with curiosity.

"Now get up. Take the panties off and come to me."

She comes to me completely naked.

"I want you to bring your pussy as close to my face as you can. Yessss…like that. I can feel the heat coming from your pussy."

I smell her scent and it's like electricity in my brain. I've been starving for her. I start stroking my cock faster and faster.

"Fuck, I need to taste you. Guide my head to your pussy."

She lifts one foot over my head and rests it on the chair back, so I get a better view of her swollen folds. I stare mesmerized at her open pussy. It is dripping with her arousal. Gently, she thrusts her pussy towards my hot willing mouth. I bury my mouth in her open sex, and I eat that sweet pussy.

Her hands grip my head. "Yes, yes, yes," she hisses, her voice is thick with lust.

I push my tongue deep into her entrance. Her voice becomes guttural. She's almost there. I can feel it in the blood throbbing in her clit. Suddenly, she moves her pussy away from my mouth. I stare at it, only a few inches from me.

I stare hungrily as she swirls her clit with her fingers. Hell, I need to be inside her.

"You like that?" she asks.

"Fuck yeah."

"Wannna watch me fuck my pussy?"

I nod. I never expected her to talk like this. But it works. She watches me as she slides her fingers into her own greedy sheath. Her juices drip over her fingers as they flutter in and out of her own pussy.

Jesus, I'm really close to coming. I won't be able to hold out much longer.

She positions herself above my cock and inch by inch, sinks her tight pussy over it. "You're so fucking big it hurts," she whispers.

… and just like that I come. My body convulsing, as hot streams of seed that should have shot into her womb, fountain up and splash over my thighs and stomach.

I stand up.

A fantasy is all it was…It's been a long time since I've jerked off to the vision of a woman.

I shower and lie on my bed. A cool breeze blows in through the open window. I'm still too full of food, my blood feels heated, and unsatisfied. I could jerk myself off again, but I know it won't help.

I toss and turn all night, restless, and needy.

I want her for real.

CHAPTER 19

DAKOTA

"Another restaurant?" I mutter, as I close the texting app and start getting dressed. What the hell do they want us to do now? Relive last night's drama?

They don't know about us paying the check after the fact, at least, I don't think they do. I haven't heard anything to the contrary, but if they're giving us another stunt to perform, it can only mean we're still in the game.

I wish I could call Trent to see what he thinks, but I know in my heart that I shouldn't get too close to him. There's just something there, something between us, but when all is said and done—he is the enemy. I'll just wait until our meeting time. It'll come soon enough. I have the feeling he'll think along the same lines I do. Who would've thought I'd ever come to that conclusion? Not me, certainly. But we both independently decided to take the money to the restaurant.

I got a glimpse of his heart last night, and it's in the right place. The look on his face when we came across each other with the money, when he realized that we had both taken the risk of being kicked out of the game. It was worth it to see the joy and relief on Mrs. Giacomo face when we explained what happened after she swore up and down not to ever let on that she knew it was all a stunt.

"Can you see me on the cover of a tabloid, telling the world about what really happens behind the scenes of that popular reality game show called Dare Me?" she joked.

The image made us both laugh. We left as friends. We promised to go back there for dinner, but that we were never spending that kind of money or eating that much again.

"I cater for weddings too," she said slyly.

"No, we're not," we both began.

"You will," she stated confidently.

I was so embarrassed I couldn't look at Trent's face.

I realize I'm humming as I curl my hair. There isn't any dread in me, not like yesterday. I didn't know what to expect yesterday. Not that I suddenly have a magic crystal ball telling me what tonight is going to bring, but now I know that I can handle it. We can handle it. No sweat.

The big problem will come later. How am I going to eliminate Trent when the time comes?

Half the other teams are already out of the game. I couldn't believe it when I got the update last night. Another time I wanted to call Trent. I settled for calling Jenny, instead.

She took a break from the bar and took her cell to sit on the steps outside the back entrance. "Half the others didn't have the balls you two have!" she crowed, and laughed loudly in my ear.

After I hung up I realized she's right. I don't know what their stunts were, but not everybody has my motivation.

I wonder what Trent's motivation is…

"Nope," I snarl into the mirror, putting down the curling iron and looking myself straight in the eye. "Don't put yourself in his shoes. Don't try to imagine what he's in this for. Don't humanize him. It'll only make things more difficult when it comes time to crush him."

I will crush him. I'm sure of it. There's no other option.

The restaurant chosen for tonight's stunt is a large chain, so it's much busier than Mrs. Giacomo's place. When I remember her Chef's garlicky, buttery lobster, I want to knock all these clueless people's heads together and ask why they're wasting their money on generic garbage when they could be supporting such an amazing business. Maybe I should've brought my soapbox with me. I smile wryly at myself and look around for Trent.

When I catch sight of him waiting by the hostess stand, I have to remind myself again, what the stakes of the game are for me. Because God—he's magnificent. Like heart-stoppingly, arrestingly *magnificent*. And he's smiling at me, which doesn't gain me any points with the hostess, or the three waitresses who have magically found a reason to linger near him

"Hey, you. Déjà vu?" he asks with a grin.

"I was wondering if this was maybe some sort of punishment," I admit under my breath. "You know. For last night."

"They can't know. We wouldn't still be in the game if they did. Don't worry so much."

When he smiles at me like this, my heart beats faster, and I feel almost light-headed with the rush of happiness. Everything is exactly as it should be.

"It's just ten of us now," he says, eyebrows raised, pleased. "They got rid of the weak ones early on."

"Wusses," I scoff, rolling my eyes.

We both laugh.

"Excuse me?" The hostess is not amused. She looks at me with a sour expression on her pretty face. She hates me for standing so close to him and sharing a laugh. It hits me that I like it. I like knowing she's jealous. I like the idea that everyone here thinks I'm with him. That he belongs to me.

Our table is in the middle of the dining room. I can't help but feel a little self-conscious as we sit. All right—*very* self-conscious. What are we going to have to do here? Trent's trying hard to look confident, but something tells me he's just as nervous as I am.

"Give it up," I advise.

"Give what up?"

"The false bravado. You know you're just as freaked out as I am."

"If it makes you feel better," he says dryly.

I grin at him. I'm in a good mood. "Oh, come down to Earth every once in awhile, or at least pretend to be a flawed human like the rest of us."

The waitress comes by and I order iced tea.

Trent gets a beer. No wine tonight.

At least, I don't think so. We still haven't gotten further direction on what the actual stunt involves.

As if the organizers of the game were reading my mind, my phone buzzes suddenly. I scramble to pick it up off the table.

Start talking in great detail
About what turns you on.
Loudly as possible.
Make sure everybody hears you.
Start NOW!

"Oh, boy," I breathe, as I realize that mine is the only phone that went off.

"I didn't get text," he observes, looking at his phone. "What do they want you to do?"

My heart starts racing to the point of making me dizzy. My stomach tightens in a knot. I can't breathe. My face flushes almost painfully hot. "You won't believe it." I can barely get those four words out. Oh, I'm going to die. I am going to die right here at this table. How can I say that sort of stuff in front of all these diners? How humiliating. What sort of sadists are we dealing with here?

He frowns. "So? What do you have to do?"

"Oh, Lord. I can't believe I have to do this." Millions of people are going to eventually see this. Mom might end up hearing about it from one of her friends. She'll be so embarrassed, but it's better she is alive and embarrassed than—Jesus, the other alternative is so painful I can't even think it. Fine, the organizers can have their pound of flesh. I'll do it. I'll humiliate myself a thousand times if I need to.

This is all for her. Nothing is too much for her.

I have to do it fast, or else risk forfeiting. It's like standing at the edge of a pool I know is filled with cold water. I can either stand here and look at it, dreading going in, or I can jump in all at once and get it over with.

I look around me. The crowd is all roughly in the early-twenties to late-forties age range. Thankfully, no kids. I'll never see any of these people again, so what does it matter what they think of me? Hopefully they'll forget all about it by tomorrow.

"I can't tell you the last time I got laid," I say, eyes darting around.

Trent's jaw drops. "Excuse me?"

"I said, it's been so long since I got laid. *Forever.* I've been dying for a nice, slow, deep screw for the longest time." God, I'm terrible at this. Absolutely the worst. I'm not even any good at sexy talk while I'm in the act.

His eyes meet mine and the lightbulb goes off. And a huge, massive, blinding smile spreads across his face.

Oh, goody.

"Tell me more," he prompts, sitting back in his chair. "Tell me all about it, sweet Dakota."

"I hate you," I whisper.

"I know." He's smiling big enough to split his face.

I clear my throat and clasp my hands together under the table to keep them from shaking. I haven't gotten any attention from the other tables yet. "I mean, what's a girl gotta do to get a nice, deep dicking every once in awhile?" I ask, my voice raising in both volume and pitch.

"You like it deep?" he asks, raising an eyebrow.

"As deep as possible. Who doesn't? I love it…" I turn my head away, just a little, so I don't have to look at him. "I love it from behind, so I can take it as deep as it'll go."

He clears his throat and shifts in his chair.

Oh, no. He is not getting an erection right now! I'm in hell. It's official. Why don't I just die and get it over with?

"What else do you like?" he asks, his voice is growly and filled with something I've never heard in it before.

"Sometimes, I like to be tied up," I announce.

This gets the attention of two tables, on either side of us. One of them is a middle-aged couple who look slightly amused, but in a, *I can't wait to share this with my book club*, sort of way. The other couple are around my age, and the girl raises a glass of wine in my direction.

My cheeks are so hot, I'd swear they're on fire.

"What's that do for you?" Trent asks.

I notice the way his jaw clenches when he speaks, like he's struggling with something. "I don't know. I guess it's something about feeling helpless. I like feeling as if I don't have a choice but to submit to whatever a man wants to do to me. It gets me off … especially when I know it's getting him off, seeing me totally helpless. Like he can do anything he wants to my body."

Now, everybody in a two-table radius is in on it. I'll be lucky if I don't get arrested for public lewdness.

"What sort of things do you want him to do?" Trent practically growls.

"The man who has me tied up?" I ask, playing for time.

He nods slowly, his eyes never leaving mine.

Oh, sweet Jesus, he's getting more and more turned on by this. And the kicker is, so am I. I feel myself getting wet just from the way he's looking at me. "I love it when he looks at me while he strokes himself. That's such a rush, when I watch a guy pleasure himself while he's looking at my body, my … pussy."

"My God," he whispers, fists clenched. "Are your legs open wide?"

I swallow hard. "Yes." I don't know what I'm more interested in—what I'm doing to him, or the volume of murmuring going on around me. I can feel the weight of dozens of eyes on me and I want to shrink away from them, but I don't want to shrink away from him.

His phone buzzes, but he doesn't pick it up right away.

"Don't you want to see what that's about?" I ask, breathless.

He pries his eyes from mine and glances at the screen, and I get the pleasure of seeing him flush for the first time.

"Oh, no," I murmur. It can't be anything good.

"Put your foot on the table."

"What?" I stare at him incredulously. I can't believe the way my heart is pounding in my chest when he looks at me the way he does.

His eyes are stormy, smoldering, like I've never seen them before. "You heard me. Hurry. We don't have much time."

I have no choice but to slide out of my flat and raise my leg until my foot is on the table in front of him.

Using the knife on the table, Trent saws off my tights and flings it on the floor.

Thank God and all the angels I got a pedicure not long ago.

Without saying a word, or breaking eye contact, he lifts my foot in one hand, and takes my big toe into his mouth.

Sheer reflex makes me pull back, but he's too strong.

He holds my foot in place while his tongue swirls around my toe, then his cheeks hollow out as he sucks it! The whole time he keeps eyes locked with mine.

I can neither help the deep sigh that slides from my mouth when I watch him, or the fresh flood of warmth soaking into my panties. I just about resist the urge to drape myself over the chair and give in-

"What is the meaning of this?"

We both look up and see a man in a suit has rushed over to us. His face is almost purple with rage. "What do you think you're doing?" he screams.

"I—we're—"

"Out," He cuts me off. "Both out! Now!" He waits until I get my foot back in my shoe, then follows closely as we hurry through the dining room to the front door. All eyes are still on us. A few shake their heads, a few mutter choice words about how disgusting we are.

I should be embarrassed. I know I should be. What we just did was extremely improper.

Completely inappropriate.

And the sexiest thing ever!

My knees are shaking so hard, I can barely walk, and it's not from shame or nerves. It's from the memory of the look on his face, the way he measured his words, and the way his velvety tongue swirled around my toe before he drew it into his hot, wet mouth, and sucked as if it was sugar.

The pleasure he took from it was mind-blowing.

I'm so flustered I almost miss the incoming text message.

Trent doesn't. Standing outside the restaurant, he reads it aloud, "Congratulations. You are now one of six remaining teams. The jackpot has reached $300,000."

When our eyes meet, it's clear that neither of us cares about that.

Not right now, anyway.

CHAPTER 20

TRENT

I need her.

Now.

All I can smell, hear, see—is her. I can still taste her skin. I feel intoxicated.

She looks up at me with those big, innocent-but-knowing eyes and I see the deep pool of passion bubbling inside her. All she needs is someone to unlock it.

I take her wrist and drag her along the street. The first alleyway we come across, I turn into. It seems like we always end up in alleys, but it's the closest private place and there's no chance of being seen in the complete darkness between the restaurant and the building next to it. I pull her in.

"What are you doing?" she whispers, but she doesn't pull away. Her lips glisten enticingly in the dark.

"I'm not the kind of guy who leaves a woman hanging," I growl before grabbing her by her upper arms, crushing her against my body, dominating her, and doing what I've been craving since the morning we met. Her lips are warm, plump and willing. They taste sweet, of gloss and something else. The world around me stops. A million memories are made in that fiery split second. Her mouth opens, and her hands turn into claws, gripping my shirt, straining to pull me closer. When my tongue slides inside her mouth, her moan makes me throb. The ache for her is so intense it's painful. I press my erection, thick and hot, against her belly.

Suddenly, she tears her mouth away, panting. "No...we shouldn't do this." She pulls back and looks up at me. Even in the darkness, I can make out the way her eyes search my face for understanding. Permission. Absolution. It's more of a statement than a question.

"Why not?"

"Surely, it must be against the rules?"

"They can't tell us what to do," I state, stroking her face, her hair, letting my hand slide down her back until it reaches the generous curve of her ass. Her groan, deep in the back of her throat, tells me she agrees. "This is about you and me, and what I've been dreaming about doing to you."

She freezes. "Wh-what have you been dreaming of doing to me?"

I lean her against the wall and kiss her again, slower this time, deeper. The thrust of my tongue mirrors the thrust of my hips against her, driving my covered cock against her thigh. I take her hips in my hands and hold her steady. All I want to do is slide balls deep into her tight heat. The thought makes me start working her dress up over her thighs.

"Trent!" she gasps, tipping her head back against the wall.

I need no further invitation. I slide my tongue down her long, lean throat before dropping into a crouch. She freezes up, hands on the back of my head, but the action of my hands on her legs, gliding up and down her thighs, stroking her ass, loosens her up.

When I pull her panties down, she steps out of them.

I take one of her legs and put it over my shoulder, stroking from knee to hip as goosebumps rise up on her skin. I can smell her now, musky and sweet, pulling me in like a magnet. Closer and closer until my nose brushes her smooth mound and she whimpers softly. Encouragingly. My tongue darts out for a taste and she's sweeter than I ever dreamt.

Fucking heaven.

"Oooh...yes..." she breathes, jerking her hips, giving all of herself to me.

And I take it, letting my tongue lap at her swollen lips, licking up her juices, diving in between her folds until I find her clit and capture it inside my mouth.

Now she's mine.

Completely under my control. Lost in pleasure, hands pulling at my hair, breathing in short gasps, she struggles to stay quiet even as I feel her quivering under my mouth. I know she's close. I thrust my tongue into her wet heat and she clenches uncontrollably. I flick my tongue over the tip of her clit and suck it into my mouth. Her body shudders. Her words echo in my head: *I like feeling I don't have a choice but to submit to whatever a man wants to do to me.*

I bite her.

And that's all it takes for her body to go rigid, and her thigh to tighten around my back. Her hips buck frantically as her orgasm tears through her. It lasts ages, but I don't take my mouth away.

Finally, her body slumps forward. Her leg is still trembling with the intensity of her climax. "Oh, my God," she pants, leaning against the wall for support, her eyes closed, and her mouth hanging open.

I put her foot back down on the ground and stand. I'm rock-hard and a little dizzy with desire, but this is enough for now. Maybe too much, but I don't care. If we weren't in public, I'd keep going.

Especially when she opens her eyes and her lips curve into a shy smile. "That was…unexpected." Dakota straightens herself out, smoothing down her dress. She looks around on the ground for her panties.

I hold them out to her and she snatches at them, still looking down.

"I guess we'd better get out of here," I murmur. "Maybe separately would be better."

"Okay. Yes. Great. Thank you." Her hand covers her face. "I mean—I'm not thanking you for this—I mean, I am, but…"

"I know what you meant." She's so fucking adorable. For her sake, I hold back the need to throw her against the wall and slam into her. I watch her leave. My cock is throbbing painfully for her. I stand in the shadows and wait until she hails a cab and climbs into it. Then I'm out of the alley and on my way to my own car.

CHAPTER 21

"**B**oy, am I glad you're off tonight." I sit on the edge of my bed and let my body fall backwards as I speak into the phone. Stretched out on the bed I stare up at the ceiling. I know Mom is fast asleep, but I keep my voice quiet.

"Oh, no. What happened? Did you drop out of the game?" Jenny sounds deeply sympathetic, but almost like she expected this to happen.

"No! In fact, there are only six teams left now."

"Really? That's fantastic! So what's the problem? Did Mr. Gorgeous piss you off?"

"Not exactly, but he is the problem."

"Not exactly? Come on. Don't tiptoe around it. Tell Aunty Jenny."

I snort. "Excellent choice of words, since my toe had something to do with it."

"Wait…What?"

After a deep breath, then another one, I spill the entire story without leaving anything out. Okay, I leave out a few key bits, but those are things that are filed under too much information.

"Dakota!" she gasps.

"I know! You don't have to tell me what a huge mistake I made. I'm already well aware."

"I wasn't going to tell you it was a mistake, but the fact that you immediately went there, makes me a little concerned for you," she says thoughtfully.

"Actually, I don't know what I feel right now. You're right. I can't stop thinking it was a mistake, and that's not a good thing."

"Did you enjoy it?"

"Oh, God, what do you think?" I close my eyes and let myself go back to that alley for just a moment. "Was it the most romantic spot? No. Did I sort of feel trashy for letting it happen there, of all places? Yes. But it was all I wanted in the entire world at that moment. And he wanted it too. It was fast, dirty and hot, but part of me still can't believe I allowed it to happen. I've never done anything like that in my whole life. Hell, anybody could've walked in that alleyway and caught us at any time."

"Girl, you are making me seriously jealous right now."

"Sorry."

"No, you're not." She laughs.

"You're right." I laugh with her, covering my face with my hand. "Oh, I don't know what to do! I mean, he's still my competition, Jen. We're down to five other couples and us. Eventually, it'll be me and him. What do I do then? I know I won't be able to forget what happened tonight, or how much I loved it."

"And neither will he," she reminds me in a quiet voice. "Don't forget that."

"You don't think he was using me, do you?"

"Absolutely not. He did it for the same reason you did it. Because even though it was bad for business, both of you wanted to do it. The game show had nothing to do with this. You were just two people for the first time since you met in the parking lot. The sparks flew even then. When you first told me about him, do you wanna know what I thought?"

I sigh heavily. "I have a feeling you're going to tell me anyway."

"I thought it sounded like you two were perfect for each other."

"That's crazy. I hated him. He was behaving like such an entitled jerk."

"It's not crazy. I've never been more serious in my life. It was that same something that made the presenter zero in on the two of you. It was fate," she proclaims dreamily.

"You're fucked in the head."

"What's your point?"

She has me there. "Anyway, it's irrelevant. It's all irrelevant. I have to beat him. I can't keep thinking of him as, you know…a man."

"You're setting yourself up to fail. Nobody can do that after someone they really fancy just got them off in an alley."

"You're supposed to be helping me through this, not reminding me how my life is going to get even more difficult from here on out. This is the first lesson in Best Friend Basics, 101."

"Oh. Okay. Let me try again." She clears her throat, then lets her voice get breathy and high-pitched. "You can do it, Dakota! I believe in you!"

"You're the worst. You know that?"

"Just think of him as a Ken doll. Nothing down there but molded plastic!"

I burst out laughing. "Trust me. That's not the case. He's a lot, lot more than molded plastic." My body flushes at the memory of his hard, probing dick pressed against my thigh, and the way he groaned when I brushed against it.

"Please, lay it on thicker. I'm not already hating your guts over your luck," she laughs.

"I don't know that I would call it luck. More like...the natural progression of what happened because of our stunts."

"Do you know how ridiculous that sounds? Stop kidding yourself. You lucked into getting paired up with a guy who can't keep his hands off of you."

"I wouldn't go that far..."

"You don't have to," she teases. "He's already done it for you."

"Jenny!"

"And I bet he would like to go even further, if you'd let him.

No man does what he did, where he did it, and doesn't want more. Trust me, girlfriend."

She might have a point, though I'm still afraid to let myself believe it. I guess I already like him too much and I don't want to let myself get more tangled with him when there's a chance he doesn't genuinely like me back. I don't want to get hurt.

I roll onto my stomach with a groan. Leaning my head on my arm, I stare off into space. "I still can't believe I did that. It's so…"

"Hot?"

"Yeah, hot, but it's so not like me."

"Maybe this is who you are," she reasons.

"Thanks a lot," I grumble.

"Jeez, I'm not calling you a back-alley slut, Dakota. All I'm saying is, maybe you have a touch of bad girl deep down inside you, and you've been waiting for an opportunity like this to let that bad girl out. You just got excited by the taboo aspect of the situation."

"I would argue the point, but it's shocking how turned-on I became in the restaurant."

"See? You're a naughty girl at heart. I knew you had it in you."

"I wish I knew what to do now. Do you have any wisdom for me?"

"What would you do if you had an illicit encounter with a guy from work?"

"Illicit encounter at my workplace? Please. There's only old

Mr. Douglas, two married middle-aged men, Ryland who is gay, and the cleaning lady." I work at a dusty warehouse where we store stuff for people. Nobody keeps anything of value there, just old files, and stuff they wouldn't really care about if it were lost. They leave it with us because we're so cheap.

"Seriously. What would you do?" she insists.

"I guess, I would find a way to face him after it was over."

"You'll find a way to face Trent, too. Hey, he wouldn't have pulled you into that alley if he didn't want you like crazy. You said he was turned-on by all that word play in the restaurant."

"Are you kidding? He led me into half of what I said. His reaction was what turned me on to begin with."

"Ugh. I hate you so much right now," she mourns. "A hot guy, salivating over you in front of a restaurant full of people. Sucking your toe in public… Anyway, I'm getting off-track. My point is, he's probably going through something similar right now. Not regret, per se. But I'd bet he's wondering what you're thinking, if he made a mistake, how he'll face you during your next stunt. I know it's easy when you're dealing with a super gorgeous, confident guy to assume they have everything together and are just so much cooler than you, but sometimes that's not the case."

"You're a wellspring of wisdom, Aunty Jenny."

"I know," she agrees smugly.

"It must come from working as a bartender," I muse. "You get to experience so much."

"I work in a dive bar," she says dryly. "It's not glamorous."

"You know what I mean. You seem so much wiser than me. I'm always the one who's like, duh, what do I do now? And you're the one with all the sensible answers."

"You scored a few points tonight, though," she points out with a giggle. "I've never had a guy go down on me in an alley before."

"I'm never gonna live this down, am I?"

"Oh, God, no." She's still laughing when she hangs up.

My cheeks tingle with my little secret...and maybe with a little bit of pride. Just a little. A smidge. I have a dirty sex story. Me. Dakota. Good Girl Dakota has a sexy story! I'm now a woman with a past. And I don't entirely hate it.

I only wish it wasn't with him—even though I'm glad and slightly more proud because it was him in that alley with me. Why can't something fun happen in my life without strings attached? Other people get to have fun, be young and not worry about it. I can't even have a fling with a hot guy without worrying it'll cost me a million dollars and my mom's life.

CHAPTER 22

TRENT

I wonder what she's going to be like today.

I'll never apologize or go back on what happened last night. We both wanted it. She had me so turned on I was about ready to burst out of my damn pants. The innocence is what got me. I've never met anybody who's so straightforward, honest and straight, but so fucking hot at the same time.

When she talked about getting tied up...

Just remembering it as I drive to the regional airport for our next stunt has me rock-hard and wanting her again. For real, this time. I've tasted her and want more. I want everything she'll give me.

So here I am, going through the same damn mental gymnastics I went through last night. It fucking kept me awake for half the night. To the point where I hope, we won't have to do anything that involves thinking or reflexes today.

The money is still my goal. My business. My dream. I'll make it happen. A little fun in an alley doesn't erase years of hard work. We're both adults, and I'm sure I still have what it takes to eliminate her from the game when the time comes. I might not even have to. She doesn't have the balls to go through with the stunts without me pushing her along. Without me, she'll most probably drop out as soon as the last stunt is announced.

It doesn't matter if she hates me.

So why is there a sharp little twinge in my chest when I imagine it ending that way?

It's the first cold day of the year. I rub my hands together to warm them up once I step out of the car. The airport is sort of out in the middle of nowhere. Nothing around for miles.

Why would they want us out here?

I double-check the latest text, confirming the time and the place. I don't see anything outside of a hangar, but a single helicopter. There's not a pilot in sight. Also, there's no Dakota. The thought that she might bail on me today never crossed my mind until just now.

Holy shit. What if that was it last night? What if she couldn't handle it and walked away? A sick feeling settles in the pit of my stomach and the cold wind turns it to ice. I'm standing alone in the middle of an airport runway and this could be the end of the line.

If it is, I'll kick myself. I let my dream die, because I couldn't fucking control myself.

When her piece of shit car makes the turn into the lot, then down to the runway, my legs feel like they could buckle out of relief. I should've known she would hang in there. She's tough.

I wave to her.

She doesn't look embarrassed, or like she wants to avoid me.

A good thing, I guess.

"Hey," she calls out, shoving her hands into the pockets of her long, black coat. It's seen better days. "What's this all about? Do you know?"

"They wouldn't tell me anything they haven't told you," I call back.

She's smiles as she reaches me. "That wasn't true last night, when they texted us separately."

I expected her to at least look shy if she brought up last night's stunt, but she doesn't. Have I underestimated her? "True," I say softly, looking deep into her eyes.

She blushes and looks away. "Do you think there's been some mix-up or something?"

"I wouldn't have thought so."

"This is eerie."

While I wouldn't have used that word, we are alone, or practically. Just the two of us in the middle of a windswept stretch of land, freezing our asses off. I have a feeling our stunts have just been taken a notch up.

Our phones buzz.

Judging by the way she fumbles for her phone, it looks like she's desperately relieved to hear it.

Good morning Dare Me Contestant.
Please go into Hangar Three
and knock at the office door.

We both shrug. So far, so good.

"This has to be a trick," she whispers as we walk. "I mean, just like everything else so far. They get us to meet up someplace, then spring some insanity on us. It looks innocent on the surface."

Just like you, I want to add, but I bite my tongue, and hold the door open for her instead. The inside of the hangar isn't much warmer than outside, but the office should be. I hope.

She knocks at the door—a little softly, but loud enough.

"Come in," a man's voice calls.

We glance at each other. I don't have a good feeling about this all of a sudden. Dakota seems frozen to the spot, so I push open the door.

The man behind the desk is old. His skin has been weathered to leather, and even though I know appearances can be deceptive, I relax a little. His kind smile is good to see, but I notice his eyes look a little sympathetic. What does he know that we don't?

He points to a stack of clothing on a table in the far corner of the room. "I'm supposed to instruct you to put those on."

"What are those?" Dakota asks, crossing the room to examine

what's waiting there. She lets out a little gasp. "Are these wetsuits?"

"They are." He looks at me and shrugs. "I'm just telling you what they told me."

"Holy cow," she whispers, eyes wide as she turns to me. "What are we supposed to do today?"

CHAPTER 23

TRENT

"I don't like this one bit!" Dakota mumbles. She is strapped in, the way I am, with a pair of headphones over her ears and a microphone in front of her mouth.

I know there have to be cameras somewhere in the helicopter, since the audience will want to catch every heart-stopping, cringe-worthy moment of this epic disaster.

I can't admit it out loud to her, but I don't like it any more than she does. Flying in a helicopter is one thing since I don't have a fear of heights. Although, it doesn't exactly make me comfortable to be this high up in the thin air wearing a wetsuit, but knowing what we have to do once we reach a specific point of the Delaware River is a whole other thing.

I flash Dakota what I hope is a confident smile. "No sweat! Just close your eyes and it'll be over before you know it!"

"You know what else could be over before I know it? My life!"

I reach for her hand and give it a quick squeeze. It's freezing cold and clammy. "They wouldn't ask us to do anything that would kill us. You have to be smart about the way you jump."

Her head whirls around. "Smart? Smart how?"

How the fuck should I know? I have to come up with something to relieve her anxiety. "Try to fall straight up and down. Point your feet. Cross your arms over your chest."

"Have you ever done anything like this before?" She wants me to say yes. She wants it so badly.

But I'm a shit liar. "No. But you've seen stuntmen perform falls like this, haven't you?"

"Actually, no. I don't like action movies." She cranes her neck to look beneath us. We're still flying over the city, and it's a gorgeous view. The skyline is speeding toward us—or, rather, we're speeding toward it—which means the river isn't far away. Which also means we don't have much time left.

She's like a frightened animal right now, so I have to be gentle, or else risk her digging her heels in. "All you've got to do is decide to get it done and do it. I know you can."

"How do you know that?" she asks, looking at me with those wide, terrified eyes. They're about as big and round as saucers.

"Because I know enough about you to know how tough you are. You don't back down from a challenge. You didn't back down that first day, remember? When I tried to intimidate you after you hit my car?"

She lets out a nervous bleat of a laugh. "I didn't hit your car. You hit mine, but it's good to know that you finally admit you were trying to intimidate me."

"Well, yeah. But you stood up to me and threw all my words back in my face. God, I wanted to fucking throw you over my knee, pull your panties down, and tan your ass."

"You did?"

Hell, yes, I did. I look back at that morning and I can feel the same physical reaction I had then: heart pounding, blood pumping in my ears, teeth-gritting levels of frustration. "You drove me crazy. I wanted to spank you into submission, Miss Dakota Manning."

She giggles a little. "At least I know for sure now."

"I'm glad I could make you feel better about yourself." I roll my eyes, and she giggles again. Good. As long as she keeps giggling, we're okay. She has to do this. She can't back out. I'll push her out of the damned helicopter if I have to. "You see? You don't back down, even when you've got me in your face. And that's not something I can say about everybody. Or even most people."

"Really? You're not just saying that?"

"Believe me. When we have the time someday, I'll tell you all about it." I look out of the copter's window. But that time is not now. We're rapidly closing in on the river and we're going to have to make the jump soon. I can see three boats sitting out on the water, forming a sort of makeshift circle. That's where we want to end up, in the center of that circle. I can just make out the shape of divers waiting on the deck of one of those boats. They're obviously there in case we need rescuing.

"I'm pretty sure I'm gonna pee in this wetsuit," Dakota frets nervously, looking out from her side of the helicopter.

"Go right ahead, but you might want to wait until you hit the water to do it."

"Thanks," she mutters. Sarcasm practically drips from her voice. At least she sounds like herself again.

"It'll be alright. I bet you'll wanna do it again by the time it's over."

"Somehow, I doubt that."

"Hey. Haven't you ever surprised yourself? Done something completely out of character?"

She turns her head slowly, eyes meeting mine. She doesn't say a word. She doesn't have to. I know exactly what she's thinking about. I just marvel silently at the way I'm thickening at the memory of last night. Even now, in this damned stupid helicopter, when I'm about to pull the stupidest stunt ever, my fucking dick is responding to her. "There you go, then," I choke out. "You're able to surprise yourself. You can do it again, right now."

She looks down again at the river then turns to me and shakes her head, her eyes full of panic. "Trent. I'm sorry. I really am, but I don't think I can do it. I'm frozen. I can't move."

"Sure, you can. Stop telling yourself you can't."

"You don't know what you're talking about. You're not me. You don't know how I feel." Her chin quivers and her chest rises and falls faster, faster, to the point where I'm afraid she'll hyperventilate before she even takes off the headphones.

"Listen to me." I lean over and take her shoulders in my

hands. "I know you have to have a damn good reason for doing this. Right? This isn't fun and games for you. You're in this for some larger reason."

She nods, silent.

"Me, too. And that's what I'm thinking about right now... how much I need the money, and why. That's what you need to remember. Why you did this. Why it's important to you. If you keep that in mind, you'll find that there isn't anything unthinkable anymore. You'll do whatever needs to be done to get where you want to go. Just follow everything the old guy taught us to do and you'll be just fine."

She nods slowly.

"You're capable of so much more than you can imagine."

"You think so?"

"I know so. If there's anybody I know that's true for, it's you." Our eyes lock and I don't look away. I need her to know I mean it, that I'm not just saying it to get her to do what we're being dared to do. I believe she could do anything if she was desperate or motivated enough to do it. Which doesn't bode well for me in the future, but it's what I have to tap into right now, if we're going to move forward.

"Do me one favor, please," she whispers before biting her lip.

"Anything."

"Hold my hand as we're jumping. Jump with me. You can let go once we're out of the chopper, but I need you with me when my feet first hit thin air."

"I can do that." I smile, and she smiles back.

"Okay! We're all set, you two." The pilot looks over his shoulder at us. "Ready to go?"

"No, of course not," Dakota laughs nervously. "But there's not much of a choice."

Dammit, I wish I didn't like her so damn much, but she says and does all the things that twist my insides, and I just can't help myself.

We unstrap ourselves and take off our headsets. Then we sit down on the edge of the opening in the side of the helicopter with our feet along the rail. The whir of the blades and roar of the engine threaten to deafen me. There's no point in saying anything more to her, since she'd never be able to hear me. The wind whips past us, all around us.

I take her hand in mine and signal with the other, holding up three fingers. She nods. God, I hope we're not both screwed right now.

Three...two...one...

And we jump.

Her hand is wrenched from mine as our bodies fall through the air, but I can't worry too much about her in those few heart-stopping moments because I'm busy trying not to die. I take my own advice, straightening my legs and pointing my toes just before hitting the water. Even with the wetsuit, it's cold enough to make my nerve endings scream in protest. I kick my legs hard and reach the surface seconds later, then immediately look for her.

She's not surfacing.

"Dakota!" I swim in a circle, breathing heavy. Every ugly

scenario imaginable flashes through my head at once and I'm just about to dive down to look for her when her head pops up not five feet from me.

She's grinning like a maniac.

"That was amazing!" Dakota screams, laughing maniacally. "You were right! I wanna do it again!"

CHAPTER 24

I can't believe I did that. I really cannot believe I did that. That's two things in two days that I never in a million years would've imagined doing. *Ever.*

But here I am, occasionally breaking into giggles as I step out of the shower Wetsuit or not, the Delaware is the Delaware and it was freezing cold. I remember again the unbeatable thrill of falling through the air, nothing under me, and the splash as my body hit the water. That awesome, adrenaline-shot moment when I knew I had made it all right, and hadn't died on impact, or wasn't about to drown. That beautiful moment when I knew I had done it.

Trent is right. I'm pretty unstoppable when I put my mind to it.

Mom is asleep when I get downstairs. Not a surprise, since it's after dinner and she usually spends most of the evening dozing. I wonder if it makes me a bad daughter, being slightly glad she's asleep. There are times when I miss being able to live in my head without having to constantly answer questions, or check on another person's welfare. I didn't spend much time living on my own, but the two years I had to myself were nice. I felt independent. I was doing my own thing. Living in my own little apartment. Yeah, it was small but it was mine. I felt I was building a life.

But as soon as Mom got her diagnosis, I felt wracked with guilt. I was immediately sure it was my fault. There had to be something I could've done to help her stay healthy. Anything. Within days, I was back in my old bedroom.

I don't regret it, not for a minute, but that doesn't mean there aren't times when I miss living the way people my age do. Going out, drinking, dating, having little adventures. Things like what I did with Trent last night aren't in my repertoire of experiences and I don't want them in my life on a day to day basis, but it was great to test my limits.

I guess my life can be described as boring, but I never minded having to grow up faster than all my other friends, or taking on all the extra responsibility of taking care of a sick parent. It only bothers me sometimes. Like tonight. When I come home bursting with energy and adrenaline and I'm all alone. There's nobody to share it with.

The doorbell is ringing. I run out from the kitchen in time to get the door before it rings again and wakes Mom.

It's Trent.

"You!"

He's standing there on the porch, leaning against the wall beside the bell, a jackass eating cactus grin stretched on his face. Only the grin doesn't reach his eyes. His gorgeous eyes look deadly serious. "Yeah, me."

"What are you doing here?"

"I came to pick you up. There are things we need to talk about."

"I—I don't know if I can just leave." I throw a glance over my shoulder. He can't see Mom and her bed from where he's standing, but I sure can.

"You have company?"

"Sort of. Not the way you think. It's my mother."

"Ah. Mommy doesn't like you going out with strange boys." One corner of his mouth quirks up in a sexy smirk. "Especially, strange boys who ride motorcycles."

Oh, so he's brought that, has he? Sure enough, it's sitting on the curb, just as sleek and shiny as ever. "I really don't know…"

"Yes, you do." His eyes meet mine and he doesn't flinch. "You do. You need to come with me."

He's right. I do. Mom's stirring as I reach for my coat and purse. "Do you need anything, Mom? I'm going to go out for a little while, if not."

She smiles. "Go. Have fun for once." The sandwich I made for her dinner is still there, waiting, along with a pitcher of water.

"Okay, I won't be long. I promise." Can I really make that promise when I don't even know where he's planning to take me? "It can't be long," I say as we're going to the bike. "I mean it. I have to be back here for my mom."

"Sure. We won't be out all night. Just give me an hour or two. Okay?"

When he smiles at me the way he is, I can't even think of saying no. Actually, what woman in her right mind would?

Instead of answering, I swing a leg over the back of his motorcycle and link my hands in front of his navel. Before I know it, we're speeding off through the night while raw adrenaline pumps through my veins. I'd better be careful before this rush becomes an addiction.

We don't go far. Just to a motel around ten minutes from my home. By the time we pull in, I know what he has in mind. Not the most romantic scenario, and the fact that he already has a room key means he's already paid for the room, which means he's planned this out.

I don't care.

I'm glad.

I've wanted this since last night. No, since before that. Since that moment after we ran from the restaurant without paying and he stood so close to me I thought he might kiss me. That was the moment when I stopped thinking about him as the competition. The enemy.

It's almost scary how it never occurs to me to question him on anything or make even a token objection as we walk into the room and he locks the door behind us. Maybe it's the naughty, irresponsible, sexy me that he's unlocked or maybe there aren't any questions that need to be asked. We are just a man and a woman who are hungry for each other.

He pins me to the wall and his mouth is on mine before I even have a chance to look around. His big powerful body crushes me, but I don't care. I want it to. I need it to. I tangle his hair around my fingers and pull his face closer to mine, kissing him back as hard as I can, until it hurts. And even the pain is good.

And still, he kisses me, breathless and grunting. Like an animal. A dog in heat or a shark that has scented blood. His tongue sliding in and out of my mouth in time with the thrusting of his hips against me. The passion is like wildfire. So much promise, so much to come. It's so hot and savage because it has been building from the moment I set eyes on him in the parking lot.

He lets go of me long enough to peel off my coat and drop it to the floor. "You taste of cherries." His hands are under my sweater and lifting it over my head. He runs his fingers through my hair and tugs my head back so the whole length of my throat is exposed to his lustful eyes.

"Jesus," he mutters thickly, before his mouth descends.

Then his mouth is all over my jaw, my throat, the side of my neck, my collarbone. Burning me, devouring me, making my head spin and waves of delicious pleasure to course through my body. I feel his mouth suck on my throat. I know what he is doing. He is branding me. Telling the world I'm his. And I let him. I let him leave his mark on me.

"Yes...yes, please..." The words pour out of me in a raspy whisper that doesn't sound like me.

He lifts his head and looks at my neck, his eyes dark with lust and feral satisfaction. "Now you're mine," he says.

I wrap my arms around his neck and hold on tight when he

cups my butt with both hands and lifting me easily, carrying me to the bed. He lowers me and stretches out on top of me.

I clasp my hands around his neck, lock my legs around his hips, and bring him closer to the center of my wet, throbbing heat. I'm aching to draw him inside. I crave him. I slide a hand between us to take a tentative stroke of that bulge.

He groans and goes stiff. He's so hard, scary big, practically bursting out of his jeans.

Clenching his jaw, he lets out a shaky breath. "I don't know how much of that I can stand," he growls before descending on me again, leaving a trail of wet, hot kisses down my chest. His fingers hook into the cups of my bra to pull them down, exposing my nipples to his greedy eyes. I arch my back, pressing myself to his mouth, moaning his name between gasps of pleasure. I lose it then. His mouth sweeps me up into an oblivion beyond words, beyond thinking.

I lift my hips when his hands reach my waist. He helps me wiggle out of my jeans and then strokes up my legs, admiring them, trailing soft kisses from ankle to thigh which makes me whimper helplessly. My head rolls from side to side as his skilled tongue flickers over the crease between my inner thigh and my plump lips.

When he picks up the scent of my yearning, he growls like a starving animal. "Jesus, the smell of your pussy is driving me crazy," he grunts as he pulls my panties aside and tastes me again.

It's bliss, even better than the first time because now it's just us. I grind my pussy against his face and cry out. I don't have to hold it in this time. I can tell him how much I love it, how good it feels, how good my body feels when he runs his tongue between my swollen lips and around my pulsing clit.

"Yes, yes, right there," I beg, straining, hips off the bed.

Then my climax hits and I go flying over the abyss. Never in my life has my orgasms been like this. It goes on and on.

His mouth is warm on my inner thighs as he pulls my panties down and I hear the lowering of his zipper. That makes me open my eyes. I want to watch as he strips down. His body is as chiseled as I guessed, strong and muscular. I could bounce a quarter off it. Heat begins to spread again in my core, and I lick my lips in anticipation when he frees his massive dick and rolls a condom down its thick length.

He moves between my legs, and I let my eyes take in the size and strength of his shoulders, arms, chest and thighs. Our eyes lock and I see pleasure in his, and lust. Need. For me. The thought makes my fire burn hotter. When he pushes forward, pressing the bulging head through my wet entrance and slides deep inside, my eyes widen with shock.

"You're so damn big," I gasp. I've never felt so stretched and full in my life.

"You're so damn tight..." he breathes, a tick in his cheek is going crazy.

He pauses to allow my muscles to relax around him before he pulls back and pushes in again. And again. We find an easy rhythm, working together, and every sure stroke of his cock brings me closer to the edge again. I close my eyes and let him take me away. I'm his. He can do whatever he wants.

He sits back on his haunches and pulls me up into his arms. Turns out I like this position even better. The friction against my clit as he moves inside me is amazing. His mouth sucks one nipple, then the other. His big, sure hands move up and down my back, over my butt, then to my hips where he guides me up and down his length.

I sit up, pulling him to me by the back of his neck for another deep, breathless kiss.

"Fuck, you're so fucking hot," he groans as his mouth moves over my neck and shoulders, nipping, licking and sucking, his breath is hot but not the same glass melting heat building in my core. He's losing control and I love it, knowing I can do this to him that I can break through that shell of confidence and control, bring out the animal side of him that grunts as I thrust harder. This is really happening, this is us— just us, losing control in each other's arms and oh, my God...!

"Yes! Yes, Yes!" I scream as I collapse in his arms, sweaty and exhausted.

He takes his last powerful thrust and explodes deep inside me. For a long while, we stay entwined while his breathing normalizes. He touches my forehead with his. I kiss the side of his head. He kisses the love bite he put on my throat.

My fingers move to the spot I'll have to hide with makeup. "Why did you do it?"

He shakes his head slowly. "I don't know. I've never done it to a woman before."

I climb off him, suddenly achy and awkward. I hope it was alright for him. He came, but it doesn't take much for a guy to do that. He must have had dozens of women in his time. Did I measure up?

He ties off the condom and turns to me with a sheepish grin. "Sorry, about the sleazy motel. It was the closest place to your home. I was going insane. I just couldn't help myself… I had to have you. Even if it meant we had to hide out here to do it."

"I got the impression you like doing things you have to apologize for," I reply looking around the room for the first time. "It's not that bad anyway. It looks pretty typical."

"You deserve better." He's not smiling anymore. "But I didn't want to run the risk of getting recognized in a high-traffic area."

"No, no, you were right. This is just fine. Seriously." What matters more than anything is who I'm with, but I don't have the courage to say that out loud. I only cuddle up next to him and hope he understands.

"Are you sure you have to be back for your mom so soon? I have the room all night," he murmurs with his mouth against my ear.

I shiver as his breath hits my skin, but I sit up. It's time for a confession. "You told me to remember my reason back in the helicopter, remember?"

He nods.

"You were right. I do have a reason. A very important one. Although you'd be surprised how many thoughts can go through a person's head in such a short amount of time." I laugh. "Or maybe you wouldn't be surprised, since you went through the same thing."

He chuckles, nodding again. "Yeah, I'm pretty sure my whole life flashed before my eyes."

He's so different now. So relaxed. It makes him even more handsome than ever, or maybe that's just because we're naked, in bed, and he's mine right now. All mine. "My mom is the reason I'm doing all of this. It was her I thought about throughout the jump."

He touches my hand, and a frown wrinkles on his forehead. "What's the matter with her?"

Instead of looking at him, I gaze down at our hands, the way they touch. If I look him in the eye right now, I'll break down. I know I will. "Lung cancer."

"Oh, Dakota. I'm so sorry." His fingers curl around mine and squeeze gently, tenderly, and that simple gesture gives me the strength to continue.

"It doesn't have to kill her, if she can get the right treatment. You know the commercials they have on TV for those special treatment centers? They, you know, take a holistic approach to treatment instead of just pumping a person full of chemicals. Not that there's anything wrong with that, but for her it would just be a delay of the inevitable. The doctors at this center can help her. They already told her so. They have a plan in place for her care. All she needs is—"

"—the money," he finishes in a flat, toneless voice.

"Exactly."

"That's why you're going through all this craziness? Because you want to save your mother's life?"

"What else is there?" I look at him, blinking, waiting for an answer.

"I don't know. Everybody has their reason. Yours is pretty strong."

I hope he'll tell me what his is, why he needs the million dollars so badly that he's willing to humiliate himself in public.

Only he doesn't. What he does is slide his hand away from mine.

And I understand something—he wishes he hadn't asked.

Because now he knows, he'll be thinking about my mom at the end of the competition, when it's only the two of us left. He doesn't know what to do with that.

I understand something else, too…I don't want to ask him now. I don't want to know. If I can imagine something tangible, a gang of loan sharks out to get him, a family business about to go underwater, even a sick relative like mine, I might hesitate when the time comes for us to stop working together and turn against each other.

I can't do that to my mom. No matter how I feel about him, no matter how much fun I'm having and hope we continue to have because that was the best sex *ever*, I love Mom more. End of story.

"Thank you for today," I whisper instead of asking him to spill his guts.

"For what? What did I do?"

"You were kind. You could've bullied me into it. Forced me. Screamed at me. You didn't. You eased me into it and reminded me why I was there in the first place. And that I had the strength inside me to do something that absolutely terrified me. I would've fallen apart if you hadn't done that. I really would have, and I'd be disqualified by now."

"You don't know that."

"Yes, I do. I know myself. I was right there on the edge, and it could've gone either way. You pushed me in the right direction." I giggle. "Besides, you were holding my hand so tight I didn't have a choice but to jump."

He chuckles, pulling me to him. "I'm glad you did."

"If I hadn't, we wouldn't still be in the game."

"Actually, if you hadn't jumped, I was going to push you."

My mouth pops open. "You wouldn't have?"

"Since you jumped, you'll never know, will you?"

I gasp when his lips brush against my throat and send shivers of pleasure down my spine. Reflex takes over and my arms wrap around his shoulders, leaving my hands free to roam over his back.

"But I'm glad I got to see you like that," he whispers. "You looked so…happy. No, not just happy. Joyous."

"Wanna see me looking joyous again?" I murmur. He kisses my earlobe before nipping it, teasing me. I close my eyes and giving myself over to him. Like I have a choice. Like I want one.

"First, I want to eat your sweet pussy again…"

CHAPTER 25

TRENT

"Who is this person, anyway?" I shout. We're standing in a line of roughly a million people. Mostly female. Mostly laughing and squealing with excitement. It almost reminds me of waiting for an audition to get on the set of Dare Me.

Dakota turns her head slowly, then blinks as if I just lapsed into Russian. "You're joking."

"I'm not."

"You're acting like you don't know just to remind me how much cooler you are than pop culture."

"I have no time for it," I say honestly. My eyes seek out and study the parking lot-sized poster hanging from the roof of the arena, draped over the wall. A larger-than-life woman with a microphone in her hand, mouth wide open like she's in the middle of belting out a long note.

"She really doesn't ring any bells?" Dakota asks. Her voice is a cross between disbelieving and horrified.

"Sorry." I look ahead. I don't know what our stunt is going to be today, but I'm willing to bet it's going to include some kind of involvement from all these people. I frown trying to think what it could be. What do those sadists want from us this time?

""No," Dakota decides firmly. "You've heard her music. You just don't know it."

"If you say so. Why is this damn line not moving an inch?"

"It will once they open the doors, genius." She rolls her eyes and smirks.

And I just want to grab her and fucking kiss her right there.

"You've heard Eva's songs. I know you have."

"Oh, my God! Will you let it go?" I laugh and wonder what I did to deserve this impossible woman in my life. "Why does it matter so much to you?"

"Because it seems unnatural." She shrugs. "What kind of person doesn't listen to the radio?"

"A person who prefers listening to carefully curated playlists, if you must know."

"Oh. I should've guessed. You have to be in control of what your delicate ears will be subjected to."

"Why not? I only have so much time in the day for music. I listen while I'm in the car, while I'm working out, and some-times if I'm working from home." Probably best to leave out the part of my history when I listened to Nine Inches and dreamed of being a famous drummer in the world's biggest Alternative rock band. "So when I have the chance, I want to listen to music I love. Is that a crime?"

She shakes her head slowly. "If you don't listen to new music, you'll never get to discover new songs to love."

"Excuse me. Have you heard what passes for music nowadays? I'll stick to what I know, thanks."

"You're such a snob," she accuses.

"I'm not a snob."

"Are."

"You're really turning this into a kindergarten-level argument."

"What is your taste anyway?"

"Can we just leave it?"

"Jesus, don't bite my head off. I was hoping to learn a little more about you. That's all."

When she puts it that way, I feel like a dick for pushing back so hard. The line is finally starting to move into the arena, which of course means everybody behind me is screaming their lungs out with excitement. "Alternative rock."

"Seriously? You like industrial rock?"

I sigh. "What's wrong now?"

Dakota laughs, waving her arms. "Nothing, nothing, it's just that I wouldn't have guessed. Hey, I love alternative rock. Who's your favorite?"

"Marilyn Manson." No hesitation.

Her face goes blank. "You're kidding?"

"Why?"

"Because that's my most favorite singer of all time. Like, nobody else even comes close."

I smile. Who'd thought? "Really?"

"Trent, I've loved his work my entire life. I have every album. Bootleg concert videos. Books. T-shirts. The whole works."

"Have you been to see him?"

"Of course. I saw him in Boston, New York, Philly and Baltimore the last time he came through."

"Now that's dedication."

"What can I say? When I love something, nothing's too much."

The line has started moving steadily now. I glance at my mobile. No texts yet. We shuffle into the huge stadium. There are ushers directing people towards their seats.

"I can't believe they got us front-row seats!" Dakota squeals, clapping her hands as an usher escorts us to two seats in the center of the row.

"I guess they can pull all kinds of strings," I muse, looking around.

Dakota runs her hands over the sweater dress she's wearing. "I hope I look okay. We might get to meet Eva"

"You think she's going to care?" I laugh. "You're not here for her."

"I'm not here for you either, buster." She elbows me in the ribs.

I fake a groan of pain then lean down and murmur in her ear,

"That's a shame, because I was about to tell you how sexy you look in that dress. You'll keep the boots on for later, won't you?" Her breath catches, and I run my lips over her earlobe before nipping it playfully.

"Not here. What if somebody sees us?" she whispers with a breathless giggle.

"So what if they do?" I ask. Even so, I glance around. One of my greatest worries is if they know we are together and using us against each other when the competition draws to a close. That's the real threat, and just the sort of thing they would do for their all important ratings.

It's weird and very unlike me, but I wish we were a normal couple, enjoying a concert together.

She smiles up at me suddenly, an open guileless smile and the wall around my heart crumbles just a little more. I can't believe how drawn I am to that smile, that voice, that face. That body. I've had plenty of bodies attached to boring, silly, immature personalities. She's different. She's a game changer.

When my phone buzzes, my heart sinks in response. Another dare is about to start.

It's not a text from the show though, it's Eric.

Yo, man, where are you?
We need to catch up.

I can't believe I haven't thought about him since jumping out of the helicopter yesterday. My brain has been tuned to the Dakota channel for a day and a half.

Sorry, bro, it's been wild
You know I trust you to keep things in order.
Will check back in soon.
Show should be over in no time.

M y heart feels heavy when I send the message. No matter how positive I try to pretend, it's like somebody or something in the universe wants to remind me of my priorities.

"Everything okay?" Dakota asks with a worried grimace.

I force a smile. "It was personal text. Work. Nothing to do with the show."

Everything to do with the show. Damn it, couldn't he have waited a little bit? I don't need to remember how important it is for me to win. Not when I'm with her and she's smiling and looking into my eyes with such trust. I guess she knows it's still a competition. She's in it for her mother and she won't forget that—no matter how good the sex is, and it's pretty damn fantastic sex.

The lights go down and the dull roar which has been filling my ears for a half hour is replaced by ear-piercing, bloodcurdling screams of complete rapture. The roar is deafening. Even the ground feels like it is heaving.

"Jesus!" I yell at Dakota, who's wearing an ear-to-ear smile.

"No! Not Jesus! Eva!" She points to the stage, where a woman is rising up on a platform surrounded by fog machines and lights. The more we see of her, the louder the shrieking gets until it reaches a fever pitch when the woman herself steps out of silhouette and into the spotlight.

I should've brought earplugs.

I have to admit it's fun seeing Dakota swaying back and forth to the music and belting her heart out. I guess she doesn't get much time to be young and carefree, so this is nice. I don't know who's more entertaining, her or the girl onstage.

I almost miss the buzz of my phone, like a tap on the shoulder reminding me this isn't all fun and games.

CHAPTER 26

TRENT

T

Having a good time?
Have an even better one with your next stunt.
Get onstage with Eva and surprise Dakota
by singing Marry You, by Bruno Mars to her.

"What the hell?" I whisper, re-reading the damn thing three times to make sure I got it right. Get onstage? With at least two dozen security guards who look like they'd love an excuse to break somebody in half for getting too close to one of the world's biggest pop stars? They have to be kidding. Or completely out-of-touch.

A thought crosses my mind. How the fuck did they know

that I even knew the words of this particular track? I'm not a fan of Bruno Mars. I only know this song because I was best man at my buddy's wedding and had to sing the chorus with him to his bride on his big day.

The only way they would know is if they'd been stalking all my friend's social media too. Fucking bastards. I never gave them permission to look into my friend's lives. That's an invasion of privacy. Fuck them and their cold ruthlessness. I hold back the anger for the moment. None of that is important. Only completing this dare is. I'm gonna do it and take great pride in taking their money. I look around me.

Think, Trent. Think.

The rest of the audience falls away and it's just me, sitting there, sizing up my options. I can't jump on the stage because of the line of security guards standing with their backs to it, arms folded over barrel chests. That's out. I wouldn't have the first clue about how to get behind the stage, so that's out, too. I scan the setup, looking for anything that'll help me.

The lighting rig?

There's a cage of metal poles set up on both sides of the stage, which is how I assume the crew climbs up and down to adjust the lights prior to the show. It looks sturdy. Yes, it would have to be, to support everything safely. If I can make my way over to it, I'll be in good shape.

Part of me cannot believe I'm actually considering this. The store, the restaurants, even jumping out of a helicopter were nothing compared to this. The arena is full to capacity, with every visible seat taken. And I'm supposed to get up in front of them and make a complete fool of myself?

Dakota is oblivious to my tension. Her excitement of over being here has made her momentarily forget why we are really here. "You okay?" she calls out, still smiling.

I stand. "Yeah. I'll be right back."

She frowns. "Hey, where are you going?"

"I need to go to the toilet."

She gives me the thumbs up signal.

I smile back.

My heart is in my throat as I work my way down the row. When I get to the end, a man presses a small velvet box into my hand. "You'll need this buddy."

I take it and step into the aisle. It is empty except for a few stragglers who are making their way to their seats. I pretend I'm one of them, slowly inching my way up to the seats on the right-hand side of the main floor area. There aren't usually risers there during basketball or hockey games, but the organizers must put them in to add more seats for concerts. I blend in with them until we reach the stairs, then vault over one of the metal partitions separating the fans from the stage and crew.

Holy shit, I can't believe I'm doing this.

Before I can talk myself out of this crazy dare, I make a dash for one of the lighting rigs and start climbing it. *One million dollars. One million dollars. My dream.* Everything I've worked so hard for. It's all come down to this and I just have to make it happen. I'm hanging thirty feet about the ground. Shit. I shouldn't have looked down. Cold sweat breaks out on my skin. It's a long way to the ground.

Come on. You can do this, Trent.

All I have to do is keep steadily crawling along. My foot slips, and my whole body jerks and tips dangerously, but I manage to told on tight, straighten myself and keep going. I picture myself receiving the million-dollar check, smiling, happy. Eric clapping me on the back. I picture myself telling Sukie to take her money and stick it where the sun don't shine. Until my feet touch the flat ground.

Holy shit, I'm actually onstage, even if nobody can see me.

Except one of the security guards, who shouts something into his headset as he charges towards me. I can't wait around to see what he wants, so I run out in full view of the entire audience. It takes seconds for them to understand this isn't planned. Except for the guy in the cable knit sweater and cords, he isn't part of Eva's backup dance squad.

The entire audience is staring at me. My mind goes blank. *What did they want me to sing?* Damn, damn, suddenly I can't remember any of the words. I have to make this happen. *The money, Trent. The money.* The cheesy words come back to me. Sure, I can do it. I can do anything.

I point to Dakota.

Her jaw is hanging open in shock. "Trent!" she shouts, pointing back. Half-laughing, half-horrified for me. She knows exactly what I'm up to.

I've never been much of a singer, but…

"It's a beautiful night!" I call out, looking around. Guards are closing in. "We're looking for something fun to do!"

"What's happening?" Eva asks, stopping and staring at me. The music goes quiet. It's just me now, running from the guards as they approach from all sides while I'm trying to sing.

"Hey, baby!" I duck when one of them tries to net me and he sprawls to the floor. I scramble away, only to almost back into another. He gives me chase, his face red and threatening, but I dance away, nimble as a cat. He's a big guy, but he's all beef and no muscle. "I think I wanna marry you," I continue singing.

"Wait a second, guys. Wait, wait." Eva holds up her hands and shoos the gorillas away. "What are you trying to accomplish here, dude?" Her smile is wide and false.

I breathe a smile of relief. You can always trust a star who smiles like that. She's seen a way to make this work for her.

She turns to the audience. "This guy's got some serious balls, getting up here like this. I have to hand it to him. What da ya think, people? Shall we let him sing his proposal?"

The crowd goes wild. She laughs and claps, one hand holding her microphone, as applause rings out through the arena.

I can't believe this is happening.

Dakota laughs until tears roll down her cheeks.

"So, tell me," she says, turning back to me, "who are you singing to?"

"Her." I point to Dakota, who's no longer laughing and is now sinking further and further down in her seat. "I was singing to her."

Whoops, cheers and whistles fill the space as a spotlight hits

Dakota and her face fills the screens throughout the place. She covers it with both hands, which only makes everybody go wilder.

"Your lady love?" Eva asks with a wink.

"Yes. She is."

More cheering, more whistling.

"Why don't you come on up, sweetheart?" Eva motions for the guards to escort Dakota onstage.

Well, this is a turn I didn't see coming.

CHAPTER 27

DAKOTA

*N*o way, no way, no freaking way this is happening.

I don't know whether I should scream with excitement that Eva is inviting me onstage, or die of embarrassment that Trent is going to make his fake proposal to me in front of thousands of people, but I don't have a choice. I need to play along with the stunt. I can't help but think what a total riot this will be for the game show audience when they see what their idea evolved into.

The audience at the concert, on the other hand, is eating this up with a spoon. They scream, they cheer, they whistle and shout encouragement as I reach the stage, blushing furiously.

Eva gins at me.

A woman in black jeans and a T-shirt comes on stage and fixes a microphone on to Trent's face.

"Okay, Cassanova. Now's your chance to woo your girl." Eva pats Trent on the back and steps out of the spotlight.

Trent looks different. There's a lot of color in his face. He's smiling as he takes my hands. God, his palms are sweaty. Or maybe it's mine that are so slick. The band starts playing the intro to the song. "It's a beautiful night..." he sings. "We're looking for something fun to do..."

"Oh, my God," I murmur, looking up to keep from giggling like a crazed person. I'm supposed to be completely into this moment. Laughing wouldn't be the right reaction.

"Oh, baby. I think I wanna marry you."

The crowd goes nuts, screaming almost as loud as they did for Eva. It gives him confidence, obviously, because he starts moving back and forth. He's dancing. Oh, sweet everything, he *is* dancing. And he's pulling me along with him, twirling me in circles with our hands locked.

"Is it that look in your eye?" he sings. "Or...whatever the next line is...hey, baby, I think I wanna marry you."

I see Eva clapping for us out of the corner of my eye as he spins me one more time and her fans start chanting *Yes! Yes! Yes!*

I squeal when he wraps his arms around my waist, and lifting me high above his head. "Don't say no, no, no," he sings, beaming. "Just say yeah, yeah, yeah..."

He puts me on the ground. My knees are so wobbly, I'm scared I'll fall. To my surprise, he gets on one knee and pulls a blue velvet box out of his pocket. My eyes widen with shock. He pops the box open. Jesus H. Christ. The sparkle of the stone-it's so big it can't possibly be real-blinds me. I can't think. I can't speak. I can't...I just stand there frozen.

"Will you marry me Dakota Manning?"

This isn't happening. I know it's not really happening. The emotions behind it aren't there. It's all a show. We're just onstage making complete fools of ourselves. That's actually what my life has become since I told Mr. Douglas I'd have to take a two weeks off to get something done.

But man, do I wish it wasn't all fake because my heart is swelling up like a balloon about to burst. I can't take my eyes off him.

His face is lit up, more gorgeous than ever, then I'm in his arms and this is wild, but it's also perfect, too. Like the most amazing dream. Suddenly, out of nowhere, while standing in front of that sea of humanity, I wish with all my heart it were real. Because...damn it...I love him. I'm in love with this man, and I've never felt so sure of anything in my life.

I want more than anything to tell him I'll marry him. For real. Forever. But all I can do is nod because, hell, we we're playing a game. This is a Dare Me stunt.

Trent slips the ring on my finger.

My phone vibrates in my jeans pocket. Surreptitiously, I slip it out and glance at it. Five words.

Kiss him like you mean it.

"What?" Trent mouths, a frown on his face.

I throw my hands around his neck and lock our lips together. Not for a second, did I think it would become a real kiss. I thought I would just press my lips for enough time to make it convincing, then we'd part and our dare would have been completed successfully, so I'm completely unprepared for what happens.

176

The magic of the situation takes over.

His mouth opens, his tongue sweeps into mine. His hand runs down my spine and wraps around my hips. He pulls my body tightly against his, so close it feels as if we are one being. I can actually feel his heartbeat. Strong and fast. His erection, hot and hard presses into me. My brain feels like it is on fire.

Then the world stops spinning.

There is no one else but us.

Only us.

Our breaths mingling. My whole body trembles uncontrollably. My heart flutters like the wings of a butterfly. I lose myself in the most beautiful kiss ever. In the history of mankind. Nobody has ever kissed like this. It goes on and on.

Then Trent raises his head and looks down at me. His eyes are shining.

I stare into his eyes. One side of his mouth quirks upwards. I take a deep breath.

The audience thinks I just accepted his proposal and they are cheering, clapping and whistling. Eva comes over to give us both a hug. I want to thank her for being so gracious, but security is already clearing us off the stage. As far as they are concerned, we've done more than enough damage tonight. Needless to say, they surround us and lead us out of the hall.

The big guy that fell on the floor while trying to catch Trent closes the gate with a *clang*. "You're more than welcome to listen from the parking lot."

Our phones buzz at the same time:

Congratulations! You just
completed your dare successfully
and won $750,000

"I can't believe we just did that!" I laugh, breathless, as we walk across the enormous lot to where we parked beside each other. My knees still feel a little weak, and I have to lean on him. He wraps an arm around my waist and that feels good. I close my eyes for a second as my head rests against his chest and God, do I wish it were all real.

"Let it never be said I'm not willing to go the extra mile." He chuckles. "Whew. I was sure they'd arrest me for a minute there."

"Tell me about it. I thought you must've lost your mind, and then I realized what was happening. Boy, they don't pull any punches, do they?"

"No, they don't. I bet none of the others would have the balls to climb up those lighting rigs. I nearly fell a couple of times."

"Shit. Imagine if you had fallen?"

"I would have dragged my broken body to the stage," he says dryly.

I laugh. "Now why did I think you didn't know any pop music?" I tease, moving away from him and leaning against my car. "When you knew ALL the words to that song."

He rolls his eyes with a grimace. "Okay, you got me. I had to learn the words when I was best man at my buddy's wedding."

"Right, right. I'll buy that. So they chose the one thing they knew you could sing."

"They trawl thought our Facebook pages and use the information there against us, Dakota."

I frown. "True. They used it against you twice now, but not against me."

He grins. "Maybe you're such a sweetheart there's nothing to use." He pulls me into a hug, the breath from his laughter warm against the side of my neck. "Can you imagine how many videos are gonna go up online after that?"

"Oh, you'll go viral, for sure. That was some stunt you pulled." I pull back with a smile. "Remember me when you are internet famous, okay?"

He kisses the tip of my nose, and I close my eyes for that split second as my heart lets out a mournful cry.

"I'll be sure to mention you in my acceptance speech."

My heart thuds painfully. "What acceptance speech?"

"You mean they don't give awards for becoming internet famous?" He grins, touching his forehead to mine.

Oh God, I thought he meant when he won the million dollars.

CHAPTER 28

TRENT

We drive to the motel separately. I'm still so hyped up on adrenaline my knees are bouncing restlessly. I know exactly what I am going to do to her. She likes to be tied up. Well, I am exactly in the mood for that. I pick up the key from reception and go to the room first. It's another bare, anonymous room with drab curtains. Her knock is timid and tentative. I yank the door open and pull her inside.

My dick is hard and ready to fuck, but one look at her face and I know something is wrong. She is still rosy from all the excitement of the concert, but her eyes, which should have been sparkling, are sad.

"What's up?" I ask quietly.

She shakes her head, her blond hair striking her cheeks. "Nothing." She looks so sweet and innocent...and lost.

"Come on, Princess. Out with it."

"I...I was just thinking of my mother."

She's one lousy liar. "Yeah, and Sangria is a fruit salad."

She cracks a smile. "I only have one hour. My friend is taking care of Mom, but she needs to go to work. Can you make this hour special, Trent?"

I smile slowly. "Yeah. You can bet your bottom dollar I can do that."

I help her undress. When she stands before me buck naked, I stare at her, awed, my cock throbbing. She gazes up at me, her eyes enormous, her mouth parted.

'Go lie on the bed, Princess."

I watch her round peachy ass make its way to the bed, before I pull at my shirt and kick off my boots and jeans. I take down my boxers and quickly sheath myself, then I stalk up to the bed and look down at her, spread out for me. To do whatever I want with. Strange, but she's the only one I've ever wanted to own. To call mine. To keep forever.

"Now hook your elbows behind your knees, open your legs wide, and show me your pretty pussy."

She pulls her knees up and exposes all that beauty to me, even her tight little asshole. I stare hungrily at her glistening pink pussy with its triangular thatch of blonde curls above. It's leaking nectar. My mouth starts watering to taste that warm, ripe, sweet summer peach again.

"I'm gonna fuck you so hard you're gonna see stars, but first I'm starving."

I dive down between her thighs and stick my tongue as deep as it will go into her delicious depths. She gasps and makes a little sound of surprise. I lick her inner walls until her thighs are trembling uncontrollably and her head is moving from side to side and she is moaning with pleasure.

I open my mouth wide and suck her whole pussy into it, the swollen fat folds, the throbbing clit. The sensation makes her shout. Her hips buck uncontrollably.

She wants me in there, and my cock is aching to oblige, but not yet.

I suck at her inner thighs, leaving marks. Not content with those, I mark her soft, creamy white flesh with my teeth. When she is a writhing almost delirious mess of excitement and anticipation, I lift my head and look at my handiwork.

I've branded her well.

I go back to her clit and expertly bring her off. She damn near tears my hair out with the strength of the climax that roars through her. While her body is bowed and her pussy is still clenching and pulsing, I plunge my cock into her. She is hot and as tight as a closed fist.

Her eyes snap open with shock.

I bend forward and take a nipple in my mouth. Like a warm little animal she pushes her breast deeper into my mouth. I run my hands over her curves and her body jerks against mine. She lets out a strange cry of frustration. I know what it is. It's the high from the concert.

She wants it as rough and wild as I do.

I know I want to fuck her so hard she'll be too sore to sit. I thrust so deep into her, her body shoots along the bed. I grab her hands by her wrists and pin them down above her head. I look down at her under me; open wide, impaled on my cock, and completely helpless. And suddenly I'm filled with a primitive need to claim sexual ownership. She is mine. Her body is mine and only mine. No other may even look at her.

"Who do you belong to?" My voice is a ferocious snarl.

Her pussy clenches at my words. "You," she whimpers.

I thrust again, harder. I want in, deep. I want to be deeper than any other man has been. I glance down to where we are joined, where my cock is slamming again and again into her pussy. Just watching my cock oiled with her cream slide in and out of her takes me to the edge. I know I can't last much longer. I feel my balls draw up and clench. A crazy thought flashes into my mind. *I need to empty my cum into her.*

I climax while thinking of my bare cock filling her little cunt. Keeping my cock deep inside her, I start playing with her clit. Swirling the wet flesh as I watch her face.

"Are you going to make me climax again?" she whispers.

"Yeah, baby, that's exactly what I'm going to do."

I take her two more times. While I've got her on her knees, her face on the pillow and her ass in the air, I pepper kisses along her spine.

"I have to go now," she mumbles reluctantly.

"Sure, you can't ask your friend to stay a bit longer?" I lick the sweat on her skin.

"No. She has to get to work. Are you licking my skin."

"Yup." I slip two fingers into her pussy.

"Don't," she protests, but she's loving it.

Lazily, I move my fingers in and out of her.

"Trent," she warns, but I notice she doesn't move away.

I tip her on her back and swoop down on her. She going home, but not before I've had my dinner and dessert.

Finally, I lie back on the bed and watch her dress. Her movements are quick. When she has pulled on her coat I experience a strange thing. A strong reluctance to let her leave. To keep her with me.

"Right, bye," she says, and again that sadness comes back to her eyes.

I get out of bed and kiss her. "Drive safely."

She nods and looks as if she is about to say something, but changes her mind and says, "You too."

Then she is gone. Leaving only her warm, intoxicating scent behind.

CHAPTER 29

DAKOTA

The first thing to filter through my consciousness the next morning is the sound of my text alert.

"Oh, come on. Have a heart," I grumble as I pull the pillow over my head. I'm in no mood right now. My eyes are still scratchy and sore from all the crying I did last night. I'm surprised the pillow isn't still damp.

This whole thing is killing me. It's become too much. Sure, winning the money is still the most important thing I have to do, and I do plan to do it, but the feelings I have for Trent have grown so much, now I feel almost unable to function. It's actually holding me back from feeling excited over what that message holds for me. I know we have to be near the end of the competition by now, and I know the next one will most probably be the stunt that pits us against each other. Why does it have to be him?

Anybody but him.

When I close my eyes, all I can see is him, smiling up at me as he twirled me around the stage, holding my body close to his.

And damned if my heart doesn't swell just the way it did last night. The pain of being in love and having to hold back is worse than anything I've ever experienced. All I want is to throw my arms around his neck, kiss him, and tell him what he means to me, but I have to pretend he's nothing because now, I'm going to have to treat him as the enemy.

Because there's Mom, and she trumps him every time. She needs me and I need her to get better, so I don't have a choice. When did I make the mistake of getting all tangled up? Mom deserves somebody better than me to fight for her. Somebody stronger, smarter. Somebody who won't let their hormones get in the way of what needs to be done. Oh, I'm so disappointed in myself for falling for him.

For wishing he fell for me, too.

Hence, the hours of crying.

The phone buzzes a second time, reminding me that I have a message waiting. I want to throw the thing out the window and forget it exists—instead, I reach out and pull it under the pillow with me.

Congratulations! You've made it to the end
Only your team remains in the competition,
after the other team couldn't complete a stunt involving a jar of spiders.
Join us in the studio today at 3:00 o'clock sharp for the taping of the finale.
Only one stunt stands between you and one million dollars!

Thank God, although, I'd have made mincemeat out of a jar of spiders. I close my eyes. One million dollars. Only one stunt between me and a million dollars.

No. Not just one stunt. One stunt and Trent. That's a much larger hurdle to clear.

The baby monitor crackles and comes to life with the sounds from the TV. Mom is already awake. Or still awake from last night. Hard to say. Her sleep schedule is all mixed-up since the medication tires her throughout the day. I can't lie around in bed feeling sorry for myself.

Besides, I have a TV appearance to get ready for. Something tells me the audience won't want to see a girl with dark shadows under her eyes from crying all night. Or maybe they will. Maybe it'll be just the sort of thing those sadists are craving.

CHAPTER 30

TRENT

I can't believe how heavy my feet feel as I walk from my car to the doors of the station. When did it all stop being so simple? I was on top of the world, ready to take a chance to make my dreams come true. Cocky as hell. Certain that I would take down all the competition and win the money. There was no other option.

And there's still no other option. Only my heart isn't in it anymore. What happens when I have to look her in the eye and know I'm the reason her mother can't get the treatment she needs? Is my dream really more important than a woman's life?

Have my priorities fallen that far out of whack that I'd even consider it? I thought I knew who I was. Maybe I never did. Maybe the go-go-go of the last few years has been a joke, a waste of time. What do I have to show for it? I haven't made progress, not really. I have office space but no staff except for Eric. A lot of promises from potential investors that all fell through, one after another. But giving up is for pussies and I'm no pussy.

Will that be enough to help me sleep at night when I know Dakota's mother died without treatment? Will I console myself with healthy quarterly returns when I know the only woman I've ever given a damn about hates me because I let her mother die? I don't want to end up as one of those burned-out businessmen who needs anxiety meds and anti-depressants just to function. What's the point of a successful business if I haven't led a successful life?

I step into the elevator, just like I did that first day. Only then, I was with Dakota. I had no idea what she'd do to me. Oh, if I could only go back to that day, when things were simpler. Life was black and white. Good and bad. Hard workers and the rest of the loser slobs who weren't brave enough, smart enough, or strong enough to hold onto their dreams the way I could. What if I did win the game? A million dollars and a lifetime of guilt.

Guilt—the gift that keeps on giving.

The hall was a flurry of activity. It's all the same as the first day. Yet, it feels so different?

One of the clipboard-holding assistants spots me. "You! Makeup!"

"Uh, alright. Where would I find that?"

She points me down the hall before hurrying away.

Terrific. Is Dakota going to be there, too? I can't believe how stressed I am as I walk in the direction of the makeup room. My shoes click against the tiled floor.

I open the door and there is no one there. No Dakota. I'm alone. They probably want to keep us separated before the big reveal of whatever stupid stunt they've come up with. I can't imagine what they'll have us do that will top what happened last night.

The door opens and a redhead with a huge rack walks in. She's carrying a mug of something. "Sorry, popped out to get some coffee."

"No problem."

"Anyway, my name is Karen, and I'll be preparing you." She puts her mug down and winks at me. "So this is the finale, huh?"

"How did you know?"

"We watch all the tapings from backstage. Your story is going to be huge when the show's edited and broadcasted. Get ready to be famous. Last night was epic. You nearly fell twice, didn't you? And that kiss. You were guys weren't pretending, were you?"

"What makes you think that?"

She laughs. "Wait until you see what I saw."

This just gets worse and worse.

She brushes against my arm and lingers just a little too long.

I get the message, but she might as well be coming on to a deaf man because all I can process is the image of me and Dakota having to do press junkets for the show. Tabloids will want to link us together. *Good Morning America* and *Today* will want to talk to us once the finale airs. I don't watch reality TV but I know the couples on the dating shows can become household names—until the next couple comes along, of course.

Karen carries on chatting while she finishes my makeup job, but I stop listening.

All I can think of is how much Dakota will hate me for winning.

"All done," Karen says, and pulls away the squares of tissue paper she tucked into my collar.

"Thanks.

The door opens and another assistant pops her head in. "You ready?"

I nod and give myself one more look in the mirror. *You've got this. You're unstoppable. All the work has led up to this moment.* But I struggle to pull up memories of all the late nights, the sleepless ones, the endless cycle of emails, meetings, cold calls and energy drinks and sometimes falling asleep at my desk when I just couldn't take anymore. I used to consider myself a warrior, one of the few who were willing to do whatever it took to succeed. I wore that like a badge. I used to look down on the weak ones, the men and women who let anything else get in the way of what had to be done.

Look at me now. What a joke. Only I don't feel like laughing.

I feel like I'm heading to the electric chair as I walk down the hall to the studio doors. "Where's Dakota?" I ask.

"Already inside. The producers thought it best to keep the two of you apart today."

Yeah, I bet they did. They love this. They want to milk it for every last bit of drama they can. And there's no way it's completely accidental that they kept pairing us in sexual, romantic situations. The strip tease club and restaurant scenario was one thing, but the concert? Making me propose? No, that wasn't an accident. They have to know something brewed between us. I hope for her sake, they don't take the low road and use it against us now.

The audience is waiting as I walk into the studio, and the murmuring I heard when the doors opened gets louder when they see me come in. When I step into the spotlight trained on one side of the set, they burst into applause. It's a far cry from the lackluster reception they gave us on the first day.

I don't see any of them. I barely hear them over the roar in my ears. All I see is her.

God, she's beautiful. And scared to death. She stops chewing on her bottom lip to smile.

I do the same. I wish I could hold her, tell her it'll be alright. No matter what happens, I'll find a way to get her mother treated. I would say or do anything right now, if only I could make her not hate me—as long as she doesn't hate me.

Out comes our host, looking just as insincere as ever. "Wow, wow! Finally, we have these two together again, in our studio! Come on, everybody, let's show them how much we've enjoyed and appreciated them over the course of the competition!"

The place erupts again, louder than ever. Almost ferocious, like a bunch of wild animals.

I need to get out of my head. I'll drive myself crazy if I don't. I blink against the lights in my eyes and try to keep smiling. If I can just focus on smiling, the rest will pass and it'll all be over soon.

"Before we get to the last stunt for you two crazy kids, why don't we revisit your antics? I know the audience would love to walk down Memory Lane." That cheesy grin is plastered to his face as he guides Dakota and me to a sofa off the side of a large screen.

I want to reach for her visibly shaking hands, but know I'd sign my own death warrant if anybody saw. And they'd all see. Instead, I wipe my clammy palms on the knees of my slacks and tell myself to relax. It'll all be over soon.

There we are. At the store. I'm running out in her underwear. The audience bursts out laughing. I can't help but smile, and a glance over at Dakota shows me she's doing the same thing. That was fun.

Me eating those worms. Turns my stomach even now. Ugh. Then Dakota dancing and the horrified expression on my face. Fuck, somebody would have to be blind not to see how fucking jealous I was.

The restaurant. I want to go back there. I want to go with her, most importantly. They got us through the windows, plus a camera placed on one of the tables. Probably, another pair of diners, there to keep an eye on us.

The other restaurant. Whoops and whistles from the audience as Dakota describes her sexual needs. I shift in discomfort. Her mortified groan is all I need to hear to know how she feels about this. They had cameras mounted all over the damn restaurant. At least there's comfort in knowing the manager was aware of something strange going on. I wish he would've clued me in.

The helicopter stunt. My pep talk. The jubilation on her face when she surfaced—and sweet Jesus—the relief on mine. Anybody could tell at first glance that I was already in love with the woman. I wish somebody had clued me in, because I didn't understand until just now.

Last night. Scared to death, ducking security guards, singing to her. Holding her, kissing her. She looked so happy. No wonder the girls in the crowd thought we were for real. She looked so happy. I looked so happy.

Like we were for real.

I look over at her now. Her face doesn't show any emotion, but her hands are clasped hard enough to turn her knuckles bone white. Is she thinking what I'm thinking?

The picture fades to black and the lights come back up, blinding me. The audience is enraptured, and the host looks like he might die of happiness. I don't even remember his name. Chip? It's as good as any other.

"All right, you crazy kids. Let's get to the main event. Which one of you is going to go home with a check for one… million…dollars?"

Oohs and ahhs come from the audience, as if on cue. I want to tell them to stop acting like sheep, but something tells me this isn't the time.

Chip-or-whatever-his-name-is turns to me. "Trent. You've impressed all of us with your determination—not to mention your fast thinking. The way you got around that first stunt was impressive. I have to admit, I wondered how the two of you would make it before you had your genius idea."

"Careful." I grin, turning on the charm. I signed on for it. It's part of the job. "It might go to my head."

He laughs like it's the funniest thing he's ever heard, and the sound is like nails on a chalkboard. "Alright, then. I know you're eager to find out about the last stunt we have in mind. Now, this stunt has already been voted upon by our studio audience." He looks at Dakota, still seated on the other end of the couch. "Yours as well, Dakota. Only the two of you are unaware of what you're in for."

He signals with one hand, and I can just about make out the shape of a person standing in the front row of the audience—but the lights are too bright for me to see who it is, or if it's a man or woman. I squint, waiting as the person to approach the set.

A girl. A beautiful girl. Tall, willowy, glossy dark hair, huge eyes the color of the sky at twilight. Exactly, the type of girl I would normally go for. She's wearing a tight pair of jeans with a thin, tight tank top that shows off ample cleavage. The sort of cleavage a man wants to bury his face in and forget his troubles. If I met her at a bar or anyplace else before meeting Dakota, I'd have been on her in a heartbeat.

Chip smiles cloyingly. "Trent, this is Amanda."

She gives me a little wave, wiggling her fingers while she chews her almost supernaturally full lips. Teasing, flirting.

"Your final stunt is much easier—and more enjoyable—than any of the ones you've completed thus far." He waves for me to join them.

I stand slowly. My heart is thumping hard. Dakota's eyes bore holes in the back of my head as I step up beside Amanda. I'm pretty sure I'd be able to hear a pin drop in the studio.

"Trent, your final stunt." Chip takes a deep breath. "You have to make out with Amanda in full view of everybody here right now."

I blink, waiting for more. "That's it?" I ask, glancing at Amanda, before returning my gaze to him. I don't dare look at Dakota. I can't.

"That's it," he confirms, and his smile widens. I wouldn't have been surprised if I saw fangs. He is a fucking leech.

Amanda smiles and nods slightly. Encouraging me. Even looking me up and down, appraising me, and I can tell she likes what she sees. Or she's been paid well to pretend she does. No, she does. I've seen that look before, and no woman needs to be paid to act like she's attracted to me. I know I'm fine. If I had a dollar for every time I've been told that, I wouldn't need their dirty million.

All I have to do to earn a million dollars is make out with this gorgeous, willing woman. That's it. It doesn't even have to last long. It just has to look real.

Here goes nothing.

CHAPTER 31

DAKOTA

I can't breathe. Oh, my God, I can't breathe. I'll suffocate right here on this stupid couch, on this stupid set, in front of all these *stupid*, cruel bunch of heartless people. They know how I feel and they have done this deliberately to torment me.

I stare at her. Gosh, she's beautiful. She's everything I'm not. Heck, I'd make out with her, and I've never done anything like that before. I can just imagine what must be going through Trent's head right now. What straight, sighted man wouldn't take one look at her and fight to keep their tongue from unrolling out of their mouth like a wolf in some old cartoon?

And he'll get a million dollars for it. That is, if I don't complete my dare. If I do, the game will just go on in this sadistic cruel vein.

I think I'm honestly going to die. The thought of him kissing another woman, for any reason, makes my heart clench so tight, it's like there's somebody squeezing it. It hurts. There's nothing stopping him, but this is all for show, just like him making out with me was for show. None of it is real. I've known it all along, haven't I?

Funny, how it doesn't even bother me that he'll qualify for the jackpot if he does it. That's the furthest thing from my mind, losing the money. It's him I care more about losing right now. It's not right. I pull myself up short. What the freaking hell is wrong with me? Mom needs me. But try as I might, I can't help thinking about him. He's slipping away from me. No, I never had him.

He takes a step closer to her, and she steps closer to him. The audience is waiting, as breathless as I am. He holds Amanda's hands in his.

I grind my teeth, hard, to keep from crying out or storming over then and punching her lights out.

Then, he looks at me. He finally looks at me.

I swallow hard.

"I'm out," he says softly.

A collective gasp fills the room. Including mine, which is probably loudest of all. He's still looking at me and now one corner of his mouth quirks up in a little smile. *It's all yours*, he's telling me. *Take it.*

I don't know if I want to laugh or cry, or smack him around for being such a dope. Why would he give up like that? Unless… No. I can't let my imagination run away with me right now. I have to keep my head on straight.

He doesn't offer an explanation, just sits back down with his hands folded and a satisfied grin on his face.

Amanda shrugs and sits back down in the audience.

I don't know what to think or say. Everybody is whispering and murmuring while looking at him, then at me.

It's all on me now.

"Trent, pal. Are you sure about this? You do understand that this eliminates you from the competition, correct?" The host glances at me before looking at Trent, who replies with a firm nod.

I can tell that this is not at all what they expected. They expected more drama for their ratings, for us to fight each other tooth and nail for the prize.

"Wow! Who would've expected this?" Chip exclaims, shaking his head. "You can't make up drama like this, folks!"

Oh, go to hell, I want to say. This is not drama. Your show just fell flat on its face.

Chip turns to me. "Now, Dakota. I wish I could tell you this means you win by default, but I'm afraid it's not that easy. You must complete your stunt, and the audience will decide when you've gone as far as you need to go."

"As far as I need to go?" I ask, looking out over the rows of seats with a sinking sensation deep in my stomach.

Oh, no. Don't tell me…

Again, he motions to the audience.

Again, someone stands and approaches the set. A tall, hunky man who looks like he belongs on a calendar or in an underwear ad. Abs I could eat breakfast off of, legs like tree trunks, arms that could squeeze a grown man to death.

I can't believe they're doing this to me.

"Alright, Dakota," Chip coos. "Same rules for you and Kurt. Try not to enjoy it too much, okay?"

The audience titters at his lame joke. Someone should kick him in the balls.

I get up, and my legs are shaky. I don't want to do this. Not in front of all of them. Not in front of Trent. I make the mistake of looking at him and he is not happy. At all. I wonder if that's because he knows he's lost, or because he doesn't want me to kiss another man. One of his hands curls into a fist and he taps his thigh with it over and over again.

Kurt flicks his hair back by tossing his head.

God, I hate men who do that.

Looking up at him is enough to give me a crick in my neck. He's so tall. This is the most awkward thing I've ever experienced, bar none. Even worse than getting my toe sucked on in public. *Come on, Dakota.* Good looking guys are usually the worst kissers, which is why Trent was such a surprise. As long as Kurt has nice breath this shouldn't be too hard. Am I seriously going to do this? Yes, I am, because I have to win. Trent has made it easy for me.

"Don't do it, honey!"

I whirl around with a gasp, searching the audience for the person that voice belongs to. She's sitting up front, next to Jenny. I could die of shame and I don't know why. And then I do. Of course, they have found her on my social media.

"Mom? What are you doing here?" My chin trembles no matter how I order myself not to cry. I go to her without thinking about it, or asking permission, and the camera crew scrambles to keep up with me.

She reaches for my hands and squeezes as hard as she can. "They picked up and brought me here. I knew you would never let me come if you knew," she explains in a soft voice. "They wanted me here for the big finale."

"Mom, I…"

She shakes her head. "I know why you did this, but I wish you hadn't. Watching those clips…"

"It was all for you, though."

"I know it was, and you're a much braver person than I am for going through with even one of those crazy stunts. I didn't know you had it in you."

"I guess I had motivation. Nothing is more important than making you better, Mom," I whisper.

"Sweetheart, you have to trust me. I've lived a lot longer than you and I know what the important things in life are. My life is worth nothing if you spoil yours."

"I'm not going to spoil my life."

"You've already put yourself out there for these people and their entertainment. I won't let you make a fool of yourself for them right now."

"It's just a kiss, Mom." I look to Jenny for help.

She doesn't say a word. She only looks at me with a slightly sad expression, which is not what I need right now.

"It won't end with a kiss," Mom adds. "It won't be that easy."

"I have to do it, Mom."

"Come on," Mom pleads. "I saw those clips. I know who you would rather be kissing right now. That's what this is about. They know how you feel about him and want to see if you'll betray him for the money. Don't let them do it to you. Stick to your guns. What's the worst that could happen?"

"I could lose." I choke back a sob. "I could lose you."

"Oh, honey, you'll never lose me."

I can't accept that. It's a nice sentiment, but it's not real life. She will die if I don't get her treated, and I can't let that happen. I let go of her hands with a smile, and walk back to Kurt anyway.

"Dakota," my mom calls, but I don't turn back to look at her.

Trent's still waiting on the couch, still staring at Kurt with a murderous light in his eyes.

When I stand next to Kurt, he turns his attention to me. I wish I knew what Trent was thinking. I wish Trent could read my thoughts. *I don't want to do this. I want to kiss you. I love you. I want us to be together when this is over. None of this is fair. Please, know that I don't want to do this.*

Suddenly, his hand unclenches, a smile comes to his face, and he nods. "It's okay. Do it. It doesn't mean anything."

He's right. It doesn't mean a thing. It's all a game. So why am I crying? I can't stop it anymore. Tears roll down my cheeks as I look up at Kurt. He looks stricken to think that a woman could be crying because she doesn't want to kiss him. Poor guy, this is going to seriously hurt his self-image. But he doesn't back down. I reach up slowly to touch his face. He's just a man. Just another man.

There isn't a sound in the studio as I stretch up on tiptoes. He leans down and we close the distance between us. I wish I could stop crying.

Ding! Ding! Ding! Ding!

My eyes fly open wide as the ringing of an alarm tears through the room and the audience bursts into applause. My head moves on a swivel, all around. What happened? They are all standing up and clapping.

"We have a winner!" The host is screaming, cheering along with the rest of them. Confetti and balloons fall from the ceiling, making it hard to see.

"What? What happened?" I ask, but my voice is lost in the commotion all around me.

"The audience has picked you as the winner with their voting devices! Congratulations!" Kurt pats me on the back and moves away, clapping along with the rest of them.

Mom is out there weeping with Jenny's arms around her.

I did it. I won. But how? I didn't even have to kiss Kurt.

I want to go to her, but I want something else more—Trent.

He stands when I turn to him and holds his arms out to me, which I gladly run into. I press my face into his neck. "I'm sorry!"

"What are you sorry for?" he asks with a laugh, holding me tight. It's heaven.

"I know how much you wanted to win," I say.

"I want you more. I want your happiness more."

I pull back and look up at him.

He's smiling as he strokes my face with a gentle, tender hand. "That's how it is when you love somebody, isn't it? You want their happiness more than you want your own."

Fresh tears fill my eyes. He understands how I feel about my mom. Then it hits me. "What? You love me?" I whisper. I'm afraid to let myself believe it.

"You are a menace on the roads, but I do love you, Dakota Manning."

"Well, you're an overbearing, arrogant jerk."

His eyebrows shoot up.

"But I love you, too. I love you so, so, so much, Trent Walker."

He lowers his mouth to meet mine and yes, this is right. This is the way it should be. His mouth closes over mine in a perfect fit, just the way our bodies fit together as we stand wrapped up in each other. Confetti floats around us and the audience screams louder than ever. It's the ending they were waiting for, I realize in the back of my mind as Trent kisses me like it's the only thing he wants to do for the rest of his life.

I can get behind that. Because it's the ending—I was dreaming of.

EPILOGUE

DAKOTA

Two Years Later

I t's a cold, clear night, and I'm glad I went against the sleeveless cocktail dress I had my eyes on for tonight. The boat is heated, but when the real show starts at midnight, it will mean stepping out onto the deck to watch the fireworks kicks off the New Year.

"This is perfect. I can't believe you got reservations!" I look around as Trent enjoys a sip of his after-dinner cocktail.

"Someone dared me," he says with a smirk, and we both laugh.

I smile at him. Sometimes, I can't believe this is my life. That anyone could be this happy. "Yeah, I know. You're a big deal."

He raises his glass in my direction before taking another sip of the amber Scotch. "Hey, you have no idea what a big deal I am."

"Oh, I think I know," I reply.

"No. You don't. I've been keeping it a secret to surprise you tonight."

I raise an eyebrow. "Uh-oh. What didn't you tell me?"

"It's good, I swear."

"Yeah, well, I'll be the judge…"

"You're tough." He smiles. "Okay, be the judge. What if I told you that you are now looking at the sole owner of the company Firedog?"

My jaw nearly hits the table. I search his face for any sign that he's pulling my chain. He's not. "How?" I gasp.

He shrugs. "Bought Sukie out. We signed the papers this morning. That's why I couldn't go out of town this weekend. And you were so pissed," he reminds me.

I lean forward. "Not pissed. Just really disappointed. I had a surprise for you."

His eyes light up. "You did?'

"I did."

"Can I still have it?" he asks eagerly.

"You can have it tonight."

He grins broadly. "Well, now that I know what I'm doing tonight."

"Actually, you don't. I told you it's a surprise," I say, pretending to be scornful.

His eyebrows rise up. "Now, I'm *really* intrigued."

"You can stay intrigued. Now back to your surprise. You should've told me!"

"Like I said, I wanted it to be a surprise." He sits back, smiling like the Cheshire Cat. "So? Surprised?"

"Extremely! I still can't believe she went for it!"

"Eh, she knew it was time to move on. She jumped on-board after the game show aired, when she saw what I was willing to go through to get the capital, but two years have passed and she's happy to cash out. She'll made ten times what she put in two years ago."

"I'm so proud of you. I wish I could jump you right now," I murmur. I've done some crazy things with him, but attacking him in the middle of a New Year's Eve dinner cruise might be too much even for ex-Dare Me contestants. Funny thing, we've never been able to live that down. Even now, we are often recognized. Sometimes, people want our autographs or just to shake our hands. They tell us that we are the best contestants that the show has ever had. All the others are pale imitations of us. Once a couple even pretended to fall in love like we did to boost up their likability score with the audience. The audience, which Trent had first thought were sheep, saw right through them.

"Ooh. Save that thought for later after my surprise."

Trent growls.

It's making me giggle. I think of my surprise and color floods up my face.

"You're blushing," he notes in wonder. "Wow, that must be some surprise you have in store for me."

I turn my attention to the beautiful skyline as we glide down the Delaware. "It looks a lot different from this angle," I murmur.

"You mean, as opposed to looking down at it from a helicopter?"

"Yes. But also…from two years later. If that makes any sense." I look at him again. "Everything looks different on this side. Like, at this time, I was desperate. I had no idea how to pay for Mom's treatment. I didn't know if she would survive, how much time we had left. I was alone except for her and Jenny. I didn't have another person in the world to lean on, or even share the happy times with."

"And now, look how everything's changed," he agrees. "Your mother's out on a date tonight, probably having a wilder time than we are."

"Oh, I doubt that very much. Mom is not doing to any guy what I am planning to do to you."

Trent laughs.

I laugh too. I know what she will be doing. She'll be dancing until dawn with her latest conquest in a Center City ballroom. Just one of a string of men falling over themselves to earn an evening with her. Beating cancer gave her a new lease on life in more ways than one. I've never seen a woman so determined to squeeze as much out of every day as she is.

"There's nothing but good times on the horizon for her," Trent says

"And if there isn't?"

He frowns. "Not the time to be negative."

"I can't help it. Sometimes I wake up in the middle of the night and my heart's pounding out of my chest because it hits me that everything is way too perfect. Doesn't that ever strike you as odd? How perfectly everything worked out?"

He shrugs. "I mean, it's not like things fell into our laps. We both worked hard before the show came along, and now we're enjoying the rewards of our hard work. We both deserve it. Besides, it's not like we're resting on our laurels now. We're still working to build our life."

"That's true." Only it doesn't quite settle the nervous fluttering in the pit of my stomach.

"Listen." He leans close, taking my hand over the table. "Life happens. We can never predict what things will look like, even a year from now. There will always be twists and turns, but the one thing you'll never ever have to worry about is us, you and me. We will always be the most important thing in my world. I am always here for you. I know we can get through anything." He chuckles. "Look what we've done so far."

His words and his smile are like a balm on my soul. He's right. We can get through anything together, so long as we're on the same team. And I know I'll always be on his team. That's something I never have to question.

He looks down at his wrist watch. "It's almost midnight. Come on. I want to see the fireworks." He gets up and tugs me out of my chair before draping his suit jacket over my shoulders.

I turn and look into his face. Mom said be grateful for the small things. Right now, I'm grateful that he never asks if I need his jacket to stay warm, or his arms to help me. It's there if I want it. The feeling of always being protected, of always being the first thing on his mind, is one I know I'll never take for granted.

He brushes his hand over the back of my neck, exposed because of the twist my hair is swept up in. He bends his and kisses the nape of my neck lightly.

A shiver runs up my spine. Even two years later, he still has that effect on me. "Can you feel the energy in the air?" I ask as we step out onto the deck. We reach the rail. Other passengers are joining us, lining up and facing in the direction of the waterfront, where the fireworks are set up.

"What does it feel like to you?" he asks, standing behind me with his arms around my waist.

Between the jacket and his warmth, I feel completely comfortable and safe. "Promise," I decide. "The promise of a fresh, new year. Anything can happen. Miracles, even. I wouldn't have guessed you were about to come into my life two years ago at this time."

"Same here," he murmurs in my ear, and his mouth brushes against the diamond earrings he bought me for Christmas.

I close my eyes for a moment and make a wish. *Please, more of this. More of him, more love, more happiness, more adventure. Whoever you are up there, please, give me more of this and I'll never be anything but grateful.*

"Ten...nine...eight...seven..." we count together, all of us on the boat and everybody standing along the water on both sides of the river. Our voices rise up like a chorus. The second we hit *'one'*, the first firework shoots up into the air.

"Happy new year!" I shout, turning to him for a sweet kiss.

There's cheering all around us, laughter and music. It's like standing onstage during the finale of the show all over again. Or at Eva's concert. The world is celebrating and it's the two of us, kissing in the middle of it, in our own world.

"Hey. I have something to ask you," he shouts over the noise from the fireworks when he pulls back from the kiss.

"What is it?" I look into his eyes and I see something there that I've wanted to see for a long time. A spark of nerves and exhilaration. This isn't going to be any old question.

He glances to the left and right, at all the people around us, and smirks. "I could've done this in the middle of a crazy scenario. A sinking ship, maybe, though that has nothing to do with the status of our relationship," he adds quickly when he sees the look on my face. "I mean, something that would reflect how we started out together. A crazy stunt. Skydiving? Bungee jumping?"

I giggle. "Oh, right. Because I would ever jump off anything after that helicopter."

"You said you loved it and wanted to do it again!"

"Yes, but that was two years ago. A lot of time has passed and I realize now that I was insane."

He chuckles. "I hope you don't feel the same way about us. That you were insane back then."

"How could I ever think that?" I'm happier than I've ever been in my whole life." This is something I tell him pretty much on the regular.

"That's good to hear, because I have something to ask you."

I forget how to breathe. I swear, this man is going to kill me one of these days because I keep forgetting to breathe around him.

He drops to one knee, slowly, drawing it out, teasing me a little.

My startled gaze drops down to him. "What are you doing?" I whisper, even though I know very well.

"What do you think?" He slides a hand into his pocket and pulls out a velvet box.

It's all happening. Everything I've ever wanted, right here in front of me. The most perfect man, somebody who loves every part of me, even the rough patches and the things I'd rather not let anybody else see. He wants to see those parts. He wants to love all of me, and I couldn't ask for more than that.

Well. Maybe a little magic. But he gives me that, too. Like right now, right in this moment, with the fireworks going off overhead, the music playing and the sparkling light reflecting in the water. Reflecting off the diamond, he reveals when he opens the box.

Holy crap, is that thing real?

"Dakota," he whispers, looking up at me with a faint smile. "You've made these two years the happiest of my life. You're the missing piece I didn't know I was missing. With you, my life is finally complete. I have a real reason to get up every day, because it's our life I'm working to build. Along with you. We're a team, the best team I could've asked for. You're everything in the world, my reason for being. And I love you with all my heart."

I cannot breathe, I just can't.

He looks down at the ring, then back up at me. "I swear to you on this ring that you'll always have every bit of me for the rest of our lives. I'll strive every day to be the man you deserve, because you deserve my best and nothing less. You will always have my devotion, support, respect, and adoration. Will you marry me?"

I can't even see anymore, my eyes are so full of tears. I'm crying so hard, I can barely move. But I can nod. I can whisper, "Yes." Once the ring is on my finger, I wrap my arms around his neck and hold onto him because my legs are too weak to support me.

As always, he holds me up. Whenever I don't think I have it in me to stand anymore, when I'm tired, frustrated, hopeless, he's the one who holds me up until I feel strong again. And he just promised to do that for the rest of his life. This wonderful, wonderful man wants me to marry him. I still can't believe I'm the one he chose, or that he chooses me everyday. The way I chose him.

"I love you," I whisper in his ear.

"And I love you," he whispers back.

It's only then that the sound of even more applause filters into my consciousness. We're surrounded by cheering passengers who slowly but surely became clued into what was happening. I hear our names called out too, which reminds me there are still people who remember us from the show.

"I guess we should be used to this by now," he whispers in my ear.

"We did sort of get our start in front of the entire country," I whisper back, holding him tighter than ever. We stay that way for a long time, wrapped up in each other, as the new year starts and we sail into it together.

Later that night…

Trent

She comes into the room wearing the little black babydoll nightie that always gets me hard instantly and holding a silk scarf. I lie in bed naked watching while my dick gets harder and harder. She stops at the bottom of the bed. Her hair is freshly washed and shiny.

"So where's my surprise?"

"You have to wear a blindfold first," she says.

I grin. "Okay."

"No taking it off until I tell you to," she says sternly.

"Yes, Ma'am."

She gets on the bed and knee-walks towards me.

Fuck, her surprise—I just want to grab her and devour her pretty pussy.

As if she can read my mind she says, "You'll regret it, because I can tell you now that you are going to love your surprise."

I let her blindfold me and fuss around checking that I can't see from under the silk.

"Right," she adds. "Remember. You can't take it off no matter what. Until I tell you to."

"Got it."

"I'm going to go out of the room and when I come back, you'll get your surprise, okay?"

"I'll be here waiting." I hear her go out and head out in the direction of the kitchen. What the hell kind of surprise has she cooked up? Intrigued, I listen until I hear her footsteps come back. I say nothing while she gets on the bed. I feel her straddle my thighs. Instantly, I'm hard again.

"My, my, you're eager," she teases.

"I'm always eager for you, sweetheart. Are you going to use that sweet little tongue of yours?"

"Maybe." She takes my cock in hand and gives it a few strokes.

Then I feel her warm tongue on the tip of my dick. She's licking my pre-cum. I groan.

I hate the blindfold, because I want to watch her. I never tire of her little cat-like licks. Her tongue moves to lick the underside of my cock and the thick vein underneath pulses. I feel thick cum dribble out of me. Suddenly, something weird happens. Whoa? Whoa! What the fuck is that? Her warm mouth is still sucking my cockhead, but something else incredibly juicy is happening too. It is wet, and wild, and fucking weird, but in a good way. In a very good way.

"How are you doing that?" I ask.

"Take your blindfold off," she instructs.

I don't need a second bidding. The blindfold is off and Goddamn, I'm staring at my woman using a grapefruit that she has hollowed out to simultaneous jack me off with while she greedily sucks my cockhead.

For a moment, I'm too surprised by the sight. I might give into the strangely fleshy pleasure or I'll laugh. I decide to give in to the fleshy-pleasure, because hell, nobody gives head like Dakota, I could lose my soul right out of my dick.

She moans around my tip as I come deep in her throat. I watch her swallow everything. She lifts her mouth from my cock and pulls the grapefruit from my dick. We have made an enormous mess. I pull her hand and she falls on top of me. I touch her cheek and she smiles at me. Her face is so innocent it makes my heart ache. I have never felt so utterly protective over any other woman before.

She looks at me from under her lashes. "And that was the grapefruit blowjob. Was it a good surprise?"

"Spectacular. Just spectacular."

The End

Interested in trying out the grapefruit technique? Follow the link for instructions. Beware the 'Darth Vader sucking up the universe' sounds though.
Have fun! ;-)

https://www.youtube.com/watch?v=wD7PKKstAcg

18704121R00129

Printed in Great Britain
by Amazon